CANDLELIGHT REGENCY SPECIAL

THE GOLDEN THISTLE

Janet Louise Roberts

A CANDLELIGHT REGENCY SPECIAL

Published by
Dell Publishing Co., Inc.
1 Dag Hammarskjold Plaza
New York, New York 10017

ISBN: 0-440-13048-4

Printed in the United States of America
Previous Dell Edition #3048
New Dell Edition
First printing—August 1978

The Golden Thistle

CHAPTER ONE

"This was an imprudent gesture, sir," said the Earl of Fitzroy with chilly hauteur. "It is a bad time to bring ladies to Rome. The Italians are ever of an unsteady, passionate nature, and the reverses of Napoleon in Russia have fired their hopes for independence."

Lady Pamela Ilchester managed to glance at her fiancé without being detected. He was a stranger to her, she reflected impatiently. He was no longer the friendly older boy she had adored as a child or the gallant wounded officer she had called upon in London. This man, so tall and dignified in his formal diplomatic garb, was an icy-tongued, frigid and aloof personage. She was not sure she even liked him anymore.

Like? She did not know him. As he argued with cold precision with her plump, bewildered brother-in-law, Sir William Granby, she studied him. Tall, red-haired, green-eyed, the Scottish burr more pronounced because he was annoyed, he was a contrast to all the others in the large drawing room of the rented Roman villa. Lady Pamela was tall, slim, and blonde—very English, said her admirers. Her sister, Lady Adelaide Granby, was also blonde, and now more plump after three children and a dozen years of marriage to a man who liked his food.

Sir Roger Saltash, aide to the Earl of Fitzroy, was nervously trying to bring peace. He probably did this often, with such a snow-covered volcano as his superior! thought Pamela. Roger was brown-haired, gallant, dreamy, kind, and Pamela had liked him instantly.

As for Lord Douglas Kinnair, the Earl whose Countess she was to be, her dislike for him was growing with every minute!

How could she ever have agreed to marry him? Matters had been different five years ago, she reflected, as she poured another cup of tea, added sugar and cream and handed it to Carlo. The Italian footman, dapper and black-haired, accepted the cup and took it over to Douglas Kinnair, who glared at the interruption. What an ill-tempered brute he was, his fiancée decided furiously. She was quite tempted to fly off.

How angry and upset poor Adelaide would be if she did! A gurgle of mischief welled in Pamela's throat. She contemplated wickedly what a lovely chaos she could create were she to rise, inform Douglas of precisely what she thought of him, break her engagement grandly, announce her immediate departure from Rome, and leave him to find some other more compliant wife when he, in his frigid fashion, should decide it was the proper time to acquire such a creature.

The frigid man was continuing his argument. It was really no good, she thought. They were here, and here they would remain. He was wrong to focus his attack on Sir William, also, for it was Adelaide who planned all!

"You see, some of the Italians are changing sides back and forth, trying to be on the winning side," said Douglas—rather cynically, she thought. "You know, my mission here was to be a secret. It seems to have joined the throng of ill-kept secrets which thrive in Rome! Nevertheless, having you come at this time, when the situation could erupt into violence, seems folly of the greatest degree." He set down his untouched cup on the mantel beside him so that the spoon clattered.

"Indeed, indeed, we saw no signs of violence. And in England, in London, we were assured—" began Sir William.

"England is confident that Napoleon will be defeated," said Adelaide calmly, nodding her head as though that settled the matter. "The Russians have him on the run. I'm sure everything will settle down to normalcy soon."

Lord Douglas turned his green-eyed stare on her, as though its fire would wither her. She smiled back sweetly.

"And we shall be late for the dinner that the Lanzas have so kindly arranged," she added, standing up. "Did you not say the reception would be at six o'clock? Have you ordered the carriages, my dearest?" she asked her husband.

"Ah—*you* did, dearest, this morning," said her harassed husband, his face purple with the upsetting situation. He was quite torn between the determination of his wife and the icy rebukes of his future brother-in-law.

For some reason, mention of the dinner engagement seemed to soothe the irate Scottish lord and he nodded abruptly. "Yes, we must be on our way. I have my carriage at the door. Shall Lady Pamela accompany me with her chaperon?"

Adelaide hesitated visibly, her desire to further the marriage speedily warring with her equally strong caution. She had set herself as guardian of Pamela since the deaths of their parents, and she took her task quite seriously.

"Ah—dearest?" she appealed to her husband for once.

"I believe it will be proper," he said solemnly.

"After all, they are formally engaged these five years."

Pamela was sure that Lord Douglas winced. Was he so reluctant then? Her fury was changing to strong dislike and embarrassment. Adelaide was wrong. He did not love her, it was *not* his duty that called him from her time and again. He did not want to marry her. She glanced down at her pretty, slim self ruefully. She was wearing a modest gown of white muslin trimmed with lilac ribbons and more lilac in the feathered headdress. Was she so unattractive to him? It piqued her vanity.

Pamela retired to her room and finished her toilette rapidly, adding a strand of modest pearls. Signora Margotti was soon knocking at her door. She entered, a tiny Italian widow of white hair and immense dignity, a sadness vying with the liveliness of her curiosity. She smiled at her young charge.

"Ah, so you are ready, so soon. The English are prompt," said the Signora. "Our ladies are inclined to dawdle about and enter late."

"Do let us speak Italian this evening; I am anxious to improve. Tomorrow we will go out again and sketch in the street. I loved that today."

Pamela snatched up her lilac cloak and was helped into it by her maid, Fanny Porter, who had accompanied them from England.

"My lady, I shouldn't think you would want to go again," said Fanny with the freedom of long acquaintance. "All those nasty mobs clustering about you, to see what you was drawing! And the streets that dirty."

Pamela only smiled. She was accustomed to taking her drawing pad with her on little expeditions. True, they had been mostly in England, sometimes in the country village which had been her home, sometimes in London, in gardens, gracious homes, and museums. It was a fresh, exciting experience to be able to sketch people and sights in the Roman streets.

"Don't fuss, Fanny," she said, picking up her lilac and gold fan. She was ready for and curious about her first glimpse of Italian society.

On the way downstairs, the Signora Margotti whispered briefly to her, "The Lanza family fought nobly against Napoleon and one of the brothers was killed. There was the father who fought, Joachim Lanza, a most honorable man, now an invalid with his wounds, God bless him. And the brothers Giuseppe and Alfonso, and of course the sister—she is named Beata."

There was a curious inflection in her tone when she came to the sister. Pamela glanced at her discreet chaperon curiously, but they were near the bottom of the stairs, and her tall, cold fiancé was waiting, an impatient look in his haughty eyes.

She wished she had kept him waiting longer!

With seeming meekness, she entered his carriage, and the chaperon took her place beside her. Lord Douglas Kinnair seated himself with his back to the horses, a gracious gesture, except that she strongly suspected he did not wish to sit next to her! So he did not care for her any more than she did for him. That was probably the real reason he did not wish her presence in Rome at this time.

Pamela chatted briefly with her chaperon on the way to the Lanza villa. Occasionally she threw a remark toward her fiancé, but she managed to invest her tone with the same coldness that he had used with her. He answered her just as briefly, glancing once curiously at her, his green eyes direct and questioning. She avoided his gaze.

To think she had once adored the boy and thought him everything gallant and honorable! At their homes, his in southern Scotland, hers in northern England, they had often met and played together when she was a girl of eight, and he a young man of eighteen. He still thought of her as a child, she assumed.

They had become engaged when Pamela was seventeen, but the marriage had been postponed until after her coming out. He had kissed her twice, both times in public under the critical eyes of her mother. Her father had already died. Then her mother had become ill and died. Adelaide had taken the girl under her wings. Pamela saw little of Douglas, as he had been posted to the Peninsula, returning badly wounded. Then she had seen him once in London before he went to his home in Scotland to recover. The next thing they had heard was that he was being sent to Rome.

Adelaide, exasperated and fearful that Pamela would be an old maid, had declared that they would follow him and expedite the wedding. Pamela had protested in vain.

She had not wanted to make a nuisance of herself when he was on a grave mission, but Adelaide had insisted. Now when Pamela thought of how he treated her—so coldly, so nastily—she thought she would rather have died than chased after him, for that was what he must think she had done.

She felt completely miserable. This was not the romantic marriage of her dreams. She furtively touched the front of her white bodice. Under it was a golden thistle brooch, his own symbol, which she had had made after their engagement. She wore it under her dress always. Romantic! He would despise her all the more if he knew.

"Here we are." The lord's grave tone was almost cheerful. He leaped from the coach and turned to help down the chaperon and then Pamela. She did not want to take his hand and hesitated so long it was obvious. His keen green eyes flashed up to meet her violet eyes. She lowered her gaze at once, touching his hand lightly to help herself alight. "You will like the Lanzas," he was saying, his keen gaze still on her face. "They are an admirable family, though their fortunes are somewhat in reverse with the Bonaparte hold here."

She replied in some suitable manner, and they went inside the lighted entrance. It was still early evening and the gardens were ablaze with October flowers of red, purple, and yellow. The villa was rather shabby, yet gracious and dignified, in gold colors reflecting the sunshine.

They were ushered into an immense living room, furnished in gold and red. Lord Douglas Kinnair went at once to the white-haired man who sat waiting for them. The man did not rise; a young man stood alertly behind his chair, ready to help him. A robe lay across his knees, though the room was not chilly. A smile lit his face and he held out both hands to Douglas, who bent to take them gently in his.

"My friend, my friend, you have come again. How gracious of you to remember old friends," he was saying excitedly in Italian.

"Remember old friends? Old comrades in arms, that is what we are; the years bringing their burdens to me also," Douglas said chaffingly. He turned to Pamela, drew her forward, and introduced her in English. She took the man's shaking hand and smiled down at him.

She could not vent her displeasure at her fiancé on such a sweet old man, she thought. She replied in her best Italian, speaking rather slowly and deliberately, but it pleased him immensely.

She was then introduced to two young Italian men of black hair and flashing eyes, and gallantly staring interest in her blond beauty. They were the sons, Giuseppe and Alfonso Lanza, and she gathered they had fought together with her future husband in battle.

Douglas asked a question. Giuseppe shrugged, flinging out his hands in the typical Italian way Pamela had observed. "Beata? Late, of course. Is she ever on time, that one?"

As he spoke, a beautiful girl entered the room and stood poised near the entrance, as though waiting for the audience to acknowledge her. Douglas left Pamela's side at once, and made his way to her, taking her hand, speaking rapidly in a low tone. She smiled up at him.

Pamela stared at them, and a pang which could only be jealousy shot through her. So this was Beata Lanza. Smooth black hair, black melting eyes, long fringed lashes: a smooth, tanned beauty in a silk dress of a plum color that emphasized her voluptuous body. Beata—the beautiful. Used to admiration, thought Pamela. The kind of woman men stared at, and flocked to.

Not a cold English beauty.

Someone Douglas admired, by the way he smiled down at her, and his husky and deep tone. She could have raged!

After that, the entire evening was a blur to Pamela. She sat silently, quite without words at Douglas's side at the dinner table. Speaking rapidly in Italian, he kept turning to his host, to Beata, to the young men—until he remembered his manners and politely translated to Adelaide and Sir William. Pamela, knowing enough Italian to understand, realized he was telling them very little of what had been said.

And always his gaze returned to Beata, poised at the end of the table, her graciousness evident in her every gesture, her words, the wave of her Italian slim hand to a waiter, the way her lashes fluttered up and down at Douglas.

So this was why Douglas was so reluctant to marry, Pamela thought finally, through the mists of resentment and misery. She could quite understand. He was enamoured of Beata, and did not want to saddle himself with a girl to whom he had become engaged nearly five years ago—and neglected ever since! She clasped her hands tightly in her lap. Her diamond and sapphire engagement ring bit into her fingers as she held her hands.

Well, she didn't want to marry him either! Deliberately, she turned to the young handsome aide at her other side and engaged him in conversation. Sir Roger was a kind man, she thought, and much, much more fun than Douglas!

Roger kindly explained some customs to her, and then they began to speak of the sketching she was doing on the Italian streets.

"I hope you do not go out alone," he asked anxiously, bending his curly brown head toward hers. "It really isn't safe, you know!"

He seemed genuinely anxious. "Oh no, I am not alone," she said lightly. "You know, the faces of the artists in the streets are quite fascinating. One agreed to let me sketch him if I would allow him to sketch me. You shall see the sketch tomorrow if you come to the villa."

Then she deftly switched the subject away from her own safety, which bored her. She longed for adventure, especially in this strange, thrilling country. She kept her attention on Roger during the remainder of the evening, and earned a rebuke from her sister before retiring. She was not repentant. Douglas had ignored her, she could ignore him!

The next morning, she was restless. She had not slept well. She went down to the library to study the latest gazettes from London and Paris. She was curled up in a large library chair reading when she thought she heard sounds.

She peeped around the large wings of the chair and caught her breath. The footman, Carlo, was systematically going through a large stack of manuscript papers from her brother-in-law's desk.

She stared! Carlo's face was no longer the bland, expressionless one of the well-trained servant. It was animated, serious, intent. Her paper rustled, and he looked up and started to his feet. He stared at her, and his hand went slowly to his pocket, then dropped. "No, I cannot attack you," he said slowly, in English. "My lady, what will you do with me?"

"You are—a *spy?*" she asked, more interested in that fact than frightened.

He stood up more erectly, then bowed. "I, Carlo da Ponte, yes, I am a spy, my lady. My country has endured much at the hands of Napoleon, and I will do anything in my power to help defeat him!"

She uncurled her legs, aware she was sitting childishly. "But we are on the same side, Carlo," she said simply. "You don't have to be afraid of me!"

"You will not—report me?" he asked slowly, uncertainly.

She shrugged. "No. You are wasting your time with my brother-in-law's papers, however. He isn't in an important post. They came here to marry me off, you know." Afterwards, she was not sure why she had suddenly confided in the Italian. Maybe because he had such large brown eyes, so gentle and devotedly wistful.

"Fate does not always deal kindly with rebels, my lady," he said simply. "But we have to fight, do we not?"

She stared, her eyes widening. "Fight? Oh—yes—yes, we do, Carlo," she whispered.

Fight? She had not even considered it, except in bitter jest. As she stared at him, the door opened and Sir William blundered in. "Oh, there you are, Pamela. Addy wants us for breakfast."

Carlo was busily dusting the papers. He darted a glance at her, in some doubt. She nodded. "Yes, just ready. I was reading the gazettes, William. Do you know, London is more interested in the latest fashions than in important things like defeating Napoleon?" She tucked her hand in her brother-in-law's arm, permitting him to escort her from the room.

CHAPTER TWO

Pamela found occasion to speak to Carlo da Ponte several times in the next few days. Her fiancé seemed so preoccupied with his secret mission, so busy and brusque, that she turned from him. What was the use of marrying him, when she could not even talk to him, she thought angrily.

But Carlo was different. One afternoon she found him dusting and straightening papers in Sir William's study. She settled down with a book in her lap, and asked cautiously:

"Carlo, will you talk to me?"

"*Si*, Signorina, if you wish," he said, with a quick cautious glance at the open door. "But you realize I cannot speak of—"

"Yes, yes," she whispered. "I won't ask you about secrets. But about Italy—talk to me about Rome. It fascinates me so much. I walk about with my chaperon, and she tells me such stories— oh, Rome is so full of history and art and beauty."

His serious young face lit up with enthusiasm. "Ah, yes," he murmured as he meticulously placed each paper on the pile, giving each one a glance, she noted. He seemed deft and very intelligent— the blank mask of a footman not disguising the very real flame of brilliance in his eyes. "Rome, the center of the world, the cultured world! I adore my Roma—my mistress. She *is* like a mistress, Signorina, if you will permit me to say so. She is capricious, loving, fiercely hating, melting, sweet, and ferocious to those who betray. She is all things to all men."

She spoke with him about that, carefully keeping her tone to a whisper. They drifted into speaking of the future of Rome, and of all the Italian states.

"When Napoleon is defeated," Carlo murmured as he dusted a shelf near her, "then Italians will rise up and throw out the foreign invaders who have violated her for centuries! Do you know that since the Roman Empire our land has been conquered and reconquered by the Austrians, the French, the Tartars—so many peoples that we cannot count them all? Yet, we are Italians, and we have a fierce love of liberty that all the torture and imprisonment and deaths cannot quench! We shall prevail!"

She stared up at him admiringly. He was bringing to life the dusty facts of her history books, the staid prose of the gazettes—talking in terms of economic appraisal and trade patterns and British rights in certain cities. Carlo had enthusiastic ideas regarding the future of Italy, and he explained them until they were interrupted by Adelaide, coming to fetch her sister for a dress fitting.

"Reading again, Pamela, love?" she sighed, ignoring the servant completely. "Really, darling, you must go out with me this afternoon and visit some people. I cannot have you brooding here alone day after day."

"I don't care for the Lanzas," said Pamela curtly. She would not soon forget the bitter evening she had spent watching her fiancé bending devotedly to every word of the divine Beata.

"Now, love, you must be practical. British marriages are not romantic. He promised to take care of you after Father died, and he will keep his word." Adelaide, for all her plump kindness and vagueness, had a shrewdness and thoughtfulness where her loved ones were concerned. She had cut to the heart of Pamela's problem. "You can count on him to marry you. He would never break an engagement or a promise."

"I almost wish he would," muttered Pamela. She saw Carlo give her a long, shrewd glance and turned away with a flush.

"Come along, darling, at least do have a fitting. You shall have some new Italian brocade dresses for this winter, and catch Douglas's eye again!"

Pamela made a rude face, and her sister shook her head. Later she returned to the study, having refused to accompany Adelaid on a visiting round, but was disappointed to find Carlo gone.

She found him again the next day, however, and they had a more involved discussion about Italian politics, the role of Napoleon, and what might happen eventually. Carlo da Ponte seemed surprised at times at the depth and breadth of Pamela's knowledge and complimented her extravagantly.

"But you have read and studied much, Signorina! What other girl, even a British girl of much education, would care to read and ponder these matters? You are so beautiful you do not need to cultivate the mind! Yet you have done so."

Douglas never complimented her; indeed, he did not seem to know she had a mind.

"But Carlo, what will really happen?"

"When Napoleon is finally defeated," said Carlo, his brown eyes glowing with fire, "ah, then. . . . You see, he has disrupted the usual pattern in Italy. For centuries, the few wealthy ruled, and also the Church. Napoleon abolished many such old traditions. Now there is a chance for work by the small tradesman, the clergy, the lesser nobility, junior army officers. We shall have a democratic form of government and prevent any one group of people from domination! And some day, some day, all of the Italian cities shall be united into one great *Italia!* I know this."

"Then Napoleon did some good here," she murmured, gazing down at her book as she heard her brother-in-law's heavy tread in the hallway. He glanced in, waved at her, and went on.

Carlo finally answered. "Yes, he shook hard the old structures, and they fell into a cloud of dust! But he is cruel, he taxes heavily. You know how he has conscripted many of our young men? Twenty thousand Italians were sent to Russia last year. How many will return? God only knows. It is a disaster what is happening there. They serve in Spain and other parts of Europe. How many return?" His tone was bitterly angry.

She looked up at him sympathetically. "The British want to help, you know," she murmured.

"Signorina, I will be truthful. The British are looking for new outlets for their trade. The Continental blockade is hurting them. Do they care about us? Do they wish us to have a democracy such as theirs? Do they want us to have rights such as they enjoy? That is my question. Or will they help us drive out Napoleon, only to coldly divide us between themselves, the Austrians, and the Germans—and anyone else who wants a piece of poor, bleeding Italy?"

They were interrupted again, but she pondered his words and spoke to him repeatedly. He was more interesting to her than all the stiff functionaries she had met in Rome. And certainly more interesting and more kind to her than her stiff, icy fiancé!

Then on a Saturday, everything broke loose. Pamela had returned early from a wearying reception and gone up to her suite of rooms. The October day had turned chilly and rainy, and the famous Roman sunlight had disappeared. She shivered and found a warm robe to slip into once Fanny had removed her muslin dress. Lord Douglas had returned with her brother-in-law and the party, and now they were in the study discussing something.

As she curled up in a large chair and stretched her feet out to rest them on a hassock, she heard shouts. She jumped up and went curiously to the door of her suite. Fanny was in the bedroom, humming as she worked. She was slightly deaf, and did not seem to hear the commotion.

As Pamela opened the door, Carlo darted past. He looked hunted, frightened. "Carlo," she hissed. "*Carlo*—here—here!"

He came toward her. "They—caught me—listening—" he panted.

"Up the stairs," shouted Lord Douglas's commanding voice. Carlo shuddered, and turned to face the front stairway.

On impulse, Pamela caught his brown wrist and pulled him. "In here, in here," she whispered.

"No, no, you will be compromised!"

"It is a life. *Your* life, Carlo. Come!" She dragged him inside her room and quietly shut the door. "Over to the window, behind the drapes—they are long."

She pushed him, as he seemed about to protest gallantly. She went with him over to the drapes, pushed him behind them, and seated herself in the chair again, picking up her book.

She heard heavy treads of the men on the stairs and in the hallway. She pretended to be absorbed. Finally there was a tap on the door.

"Come in!" she called and glanced up, expecting to see Sir William.

Lord Douglas loomed in the doorway of her drawing room, very tall, his red hair ruffled, his formal garb in disarray. His green eyes were flaming.

"Have you seen the footman, Carlo?" he asked curtly.

She drew the robe closer about her bare throat, blushing, she knew not why, except his eyes stared so at her. "Why yes, this morning," she said innocently. "I think he was downstairs. Hasn't he reported for work today?"

Douglas scowled formidably, but she gazed back at him with sweet indifference. She could find little trace in this grim businesslike man of the gentle serious boy she had known many years ago. Even the gallant, wounded officer in London had been more gay and charming than *this* man.

"He is a spy. If you see him, report at once!" he ordered, and slammed her door.

"Oh—you—" she whispered rebelliously, "if you think I will obey you, now or ever—!"

Hot fury rose as she thought of his rude behavior. She waited until the tumult seemed to be dying down, then she went over to Carlo, waiting behind the drapes.

"How can you get out? What happened?" she whispered, gazing up worriedly at him.

"I was careless. They were speaking of Lord Douglas's secret mission and I had to find out what it was. How they planned to aid the forces here, or abandon them. They caught me behind the door and I ran! It was a confession of guilt, and I am finished here."

"Oh, I *am* sorry!" She put her hand impulsively on his sleeve. He was anxious, haggard, his brown hair in curls on his forehead. He seemed so young, so vulnerable, so *gallant*. "Let me help you! The garden—if you get to the garden, you can slip out through the hedges—"

"Yes, if I can get to the garden—but how?"

She thought, then drew back the heavy drapes cautiously. There was a balcony outside, and a little drop to the terrace below. A rise in the ground made the climb not impossible—yes, it might work.

"You could drop down from the balcony," she whispered. "I will go around by the back way and stroll in the gardens. When the way is clear, I will lift my hand to my hair, and walk toward the hedges. Follow me. I will put my hand to my waist if there is danger."

She slowly repeated the directions again so they would make sure. She watched him crawl out on the balcony rail and drop down to the gardens. Then she sped out, only her robe about her.

She ran down the back stairs. "Flowers," she said, with a dazzling smile to a footman who stared at her in the lower hall. She walked more slowly out to the gardens, beautiful in the late afternoon. She paused at a group of rose bushes, touched some daisies thoughtfully, then shook her head. She glanced about. A gardener lazed in the sunshine, his back to her, apparently asleep.

Slowly she put her hand to her hair. She waited, then strolled on toward the hedges and the more elaborate formal gardens. The stables were beyond, then the woods.

She glanced back twice toward the villa, pausing as though to admire the golden hue of the ancient place, the columns and formal windows above, the russet roof of tiles, the cypress trees marching down the shaded lane toward the highway.

It was truly a beautiful, serene building, and another day she would have admired it, but today—

Carlo followed her noiselessly, creeping from hedge to hedge. Finally they reached an open space, entered it, and walked toward the fountain.

"Pamela! What are you doing out here!" The sudden deep voice in her ear, the hand closing on her wrist, made her start and cry out. She turned around to stare up at her scowling fiancé. He glared down at her, his contemptuous gaze taking in the loose, informal robe, her slippered feet, her flushed cheeks.

"Flowers," she said bravely.

Behind her, Carlo made a dart for freedom. Douglas swung about, his hand moving to the decorative sword in his belt. She caught at his hands, fiercely. "No! No! You *cannot*—" she panted, wrestling with him.

The unexpected frenzy of her attack caught him off guard. It was moments before he had pulled free, and by then Carlo was running across the area toward the trees. "Damn it to hell!" roared Lord Douglas. "Stop that man! *Stop* him!"

A stable hand stared blankly, bewildered. By then Carlo had gained the sanctuary of the trees and had disappeared.

"He got away." Douglas grasped her shoulders and shook her angrily, as though she were a child or a puppy that had disobeyed him. "How dare you interfere! He is gone—he was a spy!"

She stared back at him furiously. "I don't have to account to you for my actions! He is fighting Napoleon, fighting for his country! Yes, I would help him in any way I could!"

He glared down at her incredulously. "You did that deliberately? You knew he was a spy, and you never told me!"

She tried to wrench herself free. His fingers were cutting into her tender shoulders, and she knew she would have bruises the next day. "Let me go! Why should I tell you anything? We never talk about anything but the latest fashions. How did I know you cared at all about Italian independence?" Her head flung back, her long white throat bare, she defied him. He looked into her wide violet eyes and seemed at a loss for words.

"You—you are no longer a child," he said slowly. His hands loosened their hard hold, but he did not release her. "Tell me, Pamela, how far has this affair gone? You and that Carlo?"

"Affair?" she gasped, her eyes wider. She began to blush, her cheeks flaming with heat. She childishly put up one hand to shield her eyes from his intent gaze. "You—you wrong me! You—how dare you say—"

"How well do you know him? What contacts does he have? Do you know for certain that he is a spy?" He questioned her sternly again and again, still holding her.

She shut her mouth in a tight line, her eyes half-shut against the sunlight and glare of his green eyes. She would not betray Carlo.

"Have you had an affair with him?" he asked bluntly.

"No!" Her hand came up instinctively to slap him. He caught her hand easily, and held it tightly. "You—you are a brute and a bully! I hate you!"

"And you are a silly child. Yet—not a child. Yes, I promised," he said, as though to himself. He nodded curtly, as he had reached a decision. "Go back to the house, Pamela. I will inform Sir William that the spy got away. And as for you—I think we had best set a wedding date. I have let you run loose and get into mischief. I should have remembered your talent for getting yourself into trouble!"

"And out again!" she flared, remembering certain episodes in the past.

His grim mouth relaxed into a half-smile. "The time the black stallion ran away with you? Did you get out again by yourself?" he teased.

She almost softened, remembering how he had caught the reins of the horse, hauled her from the saddle of the brute, and carried her to safety. She had been about ten at the time.

"I have managed—most of the time," she said sullenly. "Let me go! Your hands hurt me!"

He did not let her go. He was gazing down at her as though seeing her for the first time—thoughtfully, speculatively, intimately.

"Pamela," he said very quietly, his voice deepening, "I think it best we set the wedding date. Shall we say, one month from today? Yes, I think so. The arrangements can be made for a November wedding."

She gasped, as though he had flung icy water in her face. "No—no, I don't want—"

"You don't want what?"

She stared past him, her hands going limp. She dared not say she refused to marry him. Adelaide would be so upset and angry. But everything in her rebelled at marrying this bully who alternately ignored and ordered her about. But what else could she do?

CHAPTER THREE

The next morning Pamela went to see her sister. From the lack of commotion the previous evening, she knew Lord Douglas had not revealed her role in Carlo's escape.

She found her sister in her morning room, making up menus. Adelaide looked up placidly.

"Good morning, dearest sister. Just a few minutes, and I shall be with you." She completed writing in her meticulous way, then laid down the pen.

"Dearest Addy," Pamela said coaxingly, sitting down beside her on the couch. "I wish to tell you something important. I have thought for a long time about this matter. It is not a whim or a mood."

Her sister smiled, her eyes lighting up. "I am so glad that you warned me, love. What is it now? Another violet dress?"

"No, Addy. Something much more serious. I—I do not wish—" She paused and drew a deep breath, clasping her slim hands in her lap. "Addy, I do not wish to marry Lord Douglas."

"I know that, Pamela. Nevertheless, he wishes to marry you, and he has informed me the day is set for mid-November. And you are engaged, you know, love. An engagement is not easily broken."

Pamela stared at her bland sister. Sometimes Addy had unexpected depths. "You do not realize—I do not love him," she burst out. "He is a bully and a tyrant, and he ignores me!"

"All at once? How does he bully you and ignore you, dearest?" Addy asked sweetly.

Pamela drew a deep breath once more. She rubbed her forehead. She could not confess what had happened. She searched for reasons that would convince her sister. "Well—we scarcely know each other now."

"You will come to know each other well, once you are married," Addy assured her, patting her hand. "Do not think I am callous, love! You are suffering the usual qualms of the bride. I am pleased to see them! You have been much too cool over this marriage. Now I can see that you are normal! All will go well, and you need not trouble yourself. He is of good family, of good character, and he will take good care of you! William and I are pleased with him."

"But *I* am not! He isn't at all what he seemed to be as a boy! And a young officer! He is cold and callous, he ignores me—" Pamela cried it out impetuously, her hand going to where the golden thistle lay under her dress. She really must stop wearing it, it was too romantic and silly a gesture, especially in light of the true nature of the man who had inspired it.

"Pamela, my dearest, listen to me. I think you are merely piqued that he ignores you. He is a very busy man, and he is irritated at having to plan his wedding while he is on a secret mission to Rome and I cannot blame him. So I have assured him that we will take over most of the planning, and he will not be troubled with little details. But your engagement must not be allowed to drag on and on. Why, you are already twenty-two!"

"And you reminded him of that also," flashed Pamela bitterly.

"He knows it," said Adelaide placidly. "He has known you since you were a babe. He is well aware of your age—and of his own. I delicately reminded him of his duty to provide children for his estate. He will settle down eventually."

Pamela flushed vividly at this and stared at her sister. "Oh, Addy, you didn't say that!"

"I most certainly did. He lacks a mother and a sister. I thought it my duty to remind him of certain facts. He was most gracious about it, I must say," she added complacently. Her plump hand smoothed her skirts, and she began to rise. "Well, that is settled. Now today, Pamela, the dressmaker will begin to make your wedding dress, I believe. We can set aside the formal gowns for now, she can complete them while you are on your honeymoon, then when you return, they will be in order for the occasions—"

Pamela jumped up. "Addy, how—how cold-blooded!" she blazed. "You speak of my—my honeymoon—as though it meant clothes—or—"

Addy patted her cheek. "I understand, my dearest," she told her simply. "You are upset over the wedding. Leave it to me—I shall arrange everything. And Douglas is a kind man, you need not fear him. Now, I believe the dressmaker is due to arrive— Ah, is she here now?" The last words were addressed to the maid who came in at that moment.

"The dressmaker and her assistants are in the upstairs sitting room, my lady," said the maid.

So Pamela went upstairs with her sister to be fitted and turned about and pinned into yards of material, while Adelaide chose a pattern and a fabric and lace veiling for the bridal gown. Her heart swelled with resentment, and yes—*fear*. She did not want to be married! Not like this, not to a man she did not know or understand any longer!

She must get out of it somehow. Her heart was fully resolved on that, and her resolution steeled as the hours went by. She went downstairs for lunch, thought about it, and finally after lunch caught her brother-in-law in his study.

She strove mightily to convince her plump, bewildered relative of the serious necessity of breaking off the engagement. But he could not understand.

"Pamela, dear," he said finally, "but you are having your wedding gown made! Don't you like the gown?"

It was hopeless. He was convinced that she was having a brief attack of nerves or female moodiness. Adelaide would straighten out everything, he assured her, and turned in relief to his papers and gazettes.

The October day had turned sunny and warm, and Pamela decided to escape from the villa for a time with her patient Italian chaperon. Signora Margotti was an ideal companion. She was silent when Pamela wished to be silent, she chatted in answer to her questions, she spoke intelligently about the city, and would discourse in a low voice about the present politics.

They went down one of Pamela's favorite streets in the artists' section of Rome, settling down in a café. She soothed herself by drawing and sketching the street, the profile of an artist who was frankly sketching her in return, and finally, a caricature of Beata Lanza.

She had been thinking rather angrily about the Italian beauty. She had studied her face at dinner, at a ball, at a reception, and now the lines came easily. She exaggerated the long lashes, the flirtatious look upward at a male companion, the long chin, the low-cut gown, the large bosom.

Signora Margotti glanced often at the sketch as it developed under Pamela's nimble fingers. She shook her head a little, but amusement grew at the corners of her mouth.

"You have an interesting talent, my dear," she said finally, rather frankly. "That young woman is just as you have pictured her—selfish, hard, greedy, with no love in her. But she seems to men to be all that is soft and feminine. You have seen under the skin, as we say. That sketch shows her as she is."

Pamela held it off and studied it thoughtfully. "I wondered if it was my feelings about her that made me sketch her like that. Is she really hard and selfish? But her father is so sweet—"

"Her father, yes. But she has been indulged sadly. And her mother—ah, you did not know her. Much younger than the father, grasping, climbing— Ah, I talk too much," she added half to herself, and turned a little away. "That artist group over there—I think, my lady, they might attempt to speak to you. It is time to call the carriage to us."

Pamela judged them under the fringes of her long lashes, gathered up her sketching materials, and nodded imperiously to the coachman leaning idly on a post nearby. He came over to them at once, and helped them into the carriage.

They settled themselves, and were driven down the narrow streets into the broad promenade lanes. Pamela leaned back. She was still unhappy about her impending marriage, but the outing in fresh air and sunshine had refreshed her.

She also enjoyed talking to Signora Margotti. The woman was intelligent, dignified, and thoughtful.

"We are meeting my sister at the café where we were the other day," Pamela said.

"Yes, she mentioned it. I think she is coming to enjoy our café life!" said the Signora with a smile. "Ah—I believe she is there already. Is that not she, in the blue dress and blue hat?"

Pamela smiled wickedly. "That is Addy. Surrounded by young men! Oh, if the family could see her now!" She had to chuckle. Prim, proper Adelaide was trying to shoo off the curious Roman gentlemen as one would flies, and making a poor job of it.

Pamela and the Signora alighted from their carriage and joined Adelaide, who was flushed and rather disturbed from her usual calm.

"These young men!" she said in a penetrating whisper. "They—they try to speak with me!"

Signora Margotti crisply said a few things in Italian, and reluctantly the young men drifted to nearby tables to sit and stare openly at the English ladies.

"And me with three young children," muttered Adelaide, smoothing her skirts.

"You enjoy the attentions," said Pamela calmly, as the Signora seated herself behind them at the next table. "You know you enjoy it, Addy. It is such a change from London, where you are treated as a matron. Italian men are so—so *attentive*."

"Pamela!" uttered Adelaide dreadfully, spots of color high in her cheeks. Pamela only chuckled.

"You do have a good figure yet. Plump, but Italians like plump women. They like you better than me, I am too thin for them!"

"Pamela!" It was a groan.

Pamela opened her sketchbook. "Want to see what I have been sketching?" she offered as a peace gesture.

Adelaide took the notebook with relief, glanced approvingly at several sketches, then came to Beata. "Oh dear, oh dear. You should not do this, love," she murmured. "Oh dear, it is her to the life! You really should not. She does have a long chin, doesn't she?" she added with satisfaction, stroking her own plump chin absently.

Pamela was relaxed and laughed a little as she leaned back in the white iron chair. She loved sitting in the shaded coolness of the open café drinking strong coffee rich with foamy milk. She loved being here in a new city, old in tradition and culture, where everything fascinated and attracted with its strangeness and charm. Even the Italian men, clustering about like puppies, did not annoy her. She was used to being stared at in England, but here they sighed and held their hands to their hearts, and said flattering things in Italian.

She was amused at herself for enjoying this attention. At least, some men seemed to like her looks, not like another she knew!

Then she saw them. She stiffened and stared incredulously before she caught herself and glanced away.

"What is it, Pamela?" Her sister was quick to notice. She turned in her chair, curiously. "Oh, them—" she added flatly.

Lord Douglas was driving his high phaeton

down the street at a good clip. Beside him on the high seat was a Roman beauty, her black hair half-hidden under a large plumed hat of black and ruby, her ample figure swaying on the seat. It was Beata—yes, Beata Lanza—laughing up at Pamela's fiancé. He was laughing at her also, Pamela realized.

The laugh quite changed his face. He looked younger, happier, much nicer. His face crinkled up, and his eyes were not hard, green rocks.

"You see what I have seen," said Pamela quietly to her sister, trying to stifle her fury. "It is quite impossible. To marry such a one—no thank you!"

Adelaide was visibly shaken. "They—in plain sight. Oh, in England it would not—well, others do. And he is like that. I mean, you must expect an attractive man, who has been on his own for some years— He is not a settled married man—"

"Nor will be, for me!" Pamela flashed, glancing away from the bitter sight. The phaeton was almost even with their café tables. She wanted to shrink back into the shadows, but there was no chance of it. The early blue of the evening had not yet covered them. He could see them clearly, if he but glanced in their direction.

"He is glancing in our direction," her sister hissed. "Bow, Pamela, bow and smile!"

But the obstinate girl half-turned in her white metal chair and bent her green hat devotedly in the direction of her chaperon. "Signora Margotti, what are those trees planted along the road?" she inquired sweetly.

The Signora leaned forward and answered her question, a grave look in her eyes. Pamela chatted briefly with her, then slowly turned about. The phaeton was safely down the street.

"Wicked girl," whispered Adelaide. "There would be no gossip if you would but smile and nod."

"He can go to hell," whispered Pamela with a set smile.

"Pamela!"

The waiter brought fresh coffee, but all the pleasure of the afternoon was spoiled for the girl. Her fiancé was riding about in his high phaeton with Beata Lanza. And he had told them he was too busy for outings. And furthermore, he had never taken up Pamela in his high phaeton, and she adored riding!

She burned with rage, covering it with a thin layer of politeness that deceived no one who knew her. Adelaide finally gave up trying to make conversation and sat back in resignation.

Pamela thought of her sister's words—men like that will do things like this. Yes, yes, she thought. He would marry, and continue to carry on with this Italian hussy!

And as for Douglas, he was a callous cold-blooded rascal, a libertine, a rake—

"Ah, here you are! I hoped you would remain," said a pleasant, deep voice directly behind her. She started violently.

The libertine and rake took a chair beside her, opposite Adelaide, and ordered coffee for himself calmly. At least he had the grace not to have Beata with him, thought his fiancée, furiously.

She had not spoken to him. Adelaide had greeted him with visible nervousness, earning a keen look from the green eyes.

"You have been sketching, Pamela?" he asked her, and reached out for her notebook on the table.

She shot out her hand to stop him, then remembered. "Yes, my lord," she said, very meekly. Her long lashes hid her eyes.

A lean brown hand, very large, picked up the notebook and held it, while the other hand turned over the sketches. "The artist—yes, that is good. Neatly done," he said, casually. "The street scene —ah, I think this is the street I told you not to visit?"

Silkily. Menacingly.

"Is it?" she asked indifferently. "It is a picturesque street, I think." She lifted her cold coffee to finish it.

Then he came to the sketch of Beata. His hand paused and she watched him from the corners of her eyes. Ah, that had given him a jolt!

"This is—this is extremely rude of you," he said with a chilly hauteur much at variance with his polite tone of a moment ago. "Furthermore, it is untrue. You have pictured her as—as—"

He seemed to be groping for words. She felt some bitter pleasure. "I picture people as I see them," she told him curtly.

He closed the notebook and set it down with a sort of finality. "I have been meaning to speak to you about your sketching, Pamela," he said. "I have told you not to wander so far afield. I think now I had best inform you that it is against my wishes that you should sketch in the streets at all."

He was furiously angry. And she was glad of it, glad she had penetrated his cold reserve and made him angry. At least she was able to arouse some feeling in him. Perversely, she murmured in a sweet tone, "Oh, I enjoy sketching very much. In fact, I have decided to bring my paints tomorrow, and spend the entire day with a paint brush in one of those streets. They are so colorful, you know!"

"They are not safe," he said coldly.

"I do not care about that," she said smiling, gazing straight ahead at the Roman street. Any onlooker not hearing their words would have thought they were carrying on an ordinary conversation. "I go where I please. I do what I please. If you don't like it—"

"Pamela," Adelaide said urgently. Her hand clasped Pamela's arm in a hard grip, warningly. "She is tired, I think, my lord. We should go home soon."

"Of course," he said, rising, his coffee untouched. When Pamela glanced up at him in farewell, she saw there was a tight white line about his lips, and his green eyes were blazing hot.

She felt a little thrill of fear. She had challenged him, and she had no doubt that he would find a way to meet and beat her challenge.

For the moment, she was reckless enough not to think of losing! He would find her a more formidable opponent than he had reckoned!

CHAPTER FOUR

As Douglas handed Pamela into the carriage, with a firm uplifting thrust of his strong arm, he said, "I shall see you tomorrow morning at ten o'clock, Pamela. I have matters to discuss with you."

Her mouth firmed. "But I am going out—"

She saw his eyes, and they blazed green fire. Well, perhaps this was a matter too minor to quarrel about. "Of course, my lord," she said formally. "At ten o'clock. I shall expect you."

She fumed all the way home. Why had she given in so easily? Fear? Oh, of course not! Curiosity —that was it. She was curious about what he wanted to discuss.

As for her, she had resolved on another matter.

She would not marry him. It would do no good to speak to Adelaide further about it. She would speak to Douglas himself!

She thought about it all the evening, not paying much attention to the conversation at the dinner table, nor at coffee afterwards. Adelaide cast several worried glances at her. Pamela thought she really must learn to disguise her expression—her sister could read her too easily and knew when she was plotting trouble!

But this was no frivolous scheme that Pamela intended. She was intent on much more serious matters.

She would not endure being married to a man so cold, so heartless, so enamoured with an Italian beauty that he could pay no attention at all to his own fiancée except to scold and bully her!

She thought of several approaches—hot, fiery. Or cold, contemptuous. "You, sir, are enamoured of another woman. Do you think I would marry you—"

Well, he obviously *did* think so! He thought she would put up meekly with anything he chose to do, from a mild flirtation to—well, *anything*.

Her thoughts veered hastily away from the memory of Douglas—his flaming red hair, his green eyes—bending lovingly over the dark, sleek, voluptuous form of—

No, she would not think about that. She would

simply inform him with cold courtesy that she had decided against marrying him, would have none of him, and hated him.

No, no, she must stay calm and quite collected!

"To think I once adored that hateful creature!" she informed her mirrored self incredulously. She was brushing out her long, blond hair with such vigor that it crackled. Her cheeks were flushed, her violet eyes sparkled with—hate? Yes, it must be hate.

She would amaze him with her beauty. She would wear the new brocade gown tomorrow morning, its vivid blue coloring setting off her blond—No, no. She would be simple and calm in white muslin, but with violet ribbons at her waist and in her hair. Or the pink muslin. She would be innocent and attractive—*girlish*—but he liked voluptuous Italian women with black hair and long lashes.

She went to bed, to toss and turn half the night, planning rational statements to convince him she was firmly and definitely against marrying him. She had not come to Rome to marry him, just to break the engagement. Her sister would understand and the matter would be at an end.

She blinked against tears. At an end? She had once thought she would be the happiest girl in the world if only she could marry her adored Douglas! She lay still, remembering the times they had raced their stallions against each other, how she had visited him in London after his injuries in battle. How she had wanted then to marry him, nurse him, care for his injuries, wipe out the bitter memories and the suffering which had carved deep lines on either side of his mouth. She had wanted to kiss that mouth, those firm, sensuous lines.

To distract herself from such shameful thoughts, she had chattered gaily to him, feverishly recounting all the balls and routs and gaming she had done, how she had raced her horse in Hyde Park, how furious Adelaide had been when she had torn her new gown dancing at a ball.

It was almost morning before she fell into a fretful sleep. She woke heavy-eyed to find Fanny Porter drawing the curtains and moving to the bathroom to draw her bath.

"It can't be morning," she said.

"Yes, it be, my lady. Another day, and your beau coming to see you this morning," said Fanny cheerfully.

Pamela groaned. She allowed herself to be served a cup of hot tea, which did not soothe her as it usually did. She bathed, then dressed in the first dress Fanny brought, a white muslin with violet ribbons. "Just like your eyes, my lady," said Fanny happily. "His lordship cannot help but notice."

"He likes black eyes," said Pamela glumly.

Fanny looked serious, her mouth tight. She, too, had heard the gossip, thought Pamela.

She tied up her hair in the violet ribbon, thought her eyes looked as though she had not slept, and went sullenly down to breakfast.

"His Lordship has condescended to join us for breakfast," her sister told her as soon as she entered the breakfast room.

Pamela started. Douglas was turning from where he stood at the window. The early sunshine seemed to set his Scottish red hair afire. She could scarcely see his face, as he stood with his back to the morning light.

"Good morning," she said.

He crossed to her and held her chair. She sank into it, her knees feeling weak.

"Good morning, Pamela," he said, and went to his own chair. Sir William was already heartily consuming quantities of ham, eggs, biscuits, and tea. Pamela picked at her food until warned by a frowning look from her sister. No, she would not betray her uneasiness in this way.

Douglas seemed to have a good appetite, she noticed bitterly. Perhaps nothing put him off his food.

She paid little attention to the conversation until Sir William mentioned Carlo.

"No word of that spy, Carlo? Drat the fellow. I wonder if he stole anything." Sir William attacked another piece of ham vigorously.

Pamela stole a little look at Douglas. He was gazing at her keenly, a biscuit unnoticed in his fingers. She was angry that she felt warm. She knew her cheeks showed a vivid blush.

"Very little word," said Douglas finally. "I expect he will turn up somewhere."

"Spies do not usually steal, do they?" asked Pamela innocently. "Don't they usually just—uh—look at papers, and memorize secrets, and listen at doors, and that sort of thing?"

A faint smile touched Douglas's lips. "Sounds as though you might know the business, Pamela."

"Oh—just observation. I mean, I think that would be—"

Addy interrupted placidly. "I think you have been reading too many novels, my dear!"

"Perhaps so, Addy."

Her blush died down and her irritation returned as Douglas and William exclaimed over the news of the day, exchanged trite observations on the weather, and generally spoke of nothing at all.

When Pamela had finished her tea, Douglas rose promptly, excused himself to his hostess, and conducted Pamela into the library. Once there, he closed the door.

"It is quite all right, my dear. I have the permission of your sister to speak to you alone!" he said, not reassuringly.

She took refuge in a large chair near the fireplace, and looked up at him warily. He chose to stand at the mantel, and gazed down at her steadily.

"I have something to say to you also," she said belligerently, twisting her violet handkerchief in her fingers.

"Fine. May I speak first? I wish to discuss our wedding plans. The church—"

"No," she said, stiffening. "I—what I have to say—I mean, I can't marry you!" she blurted out.

"Yes, you can," he said. "And you will!"

She had rehearsed dialogue between them and it was not going as planned. She shifted uneasily. "I mean to say, sir, that after careful consideration I have decided against venturing into matrimony —at least at this time—and therefore, I am cancelling our agreement, and our engagement is at an end!" She managed to get out the last breathless words before his gathering scowl of anger.

"That is nonsense, as you know, my dear," he said, more gently than she had anticipated. "We have been engaged these five years—"

"Too long," she blurted. "I mean," and she knew the stupid betraying color was coming up in her fine English complexion, "I mean—we no longer know each other. You have been away for years—"

"It is time we settled matters between us. I promised your father and mother I would always care for you. It is a sacred, solemn oath I swore, and I do not mean to break it. I realize we seem like strangers, yet we knew each other as children—"

"You are not at all like the boy I knew!"

He paused, gazing down at her, the frown smoothed out. "I am not a boy, Pamela. I have not been a boy since my first battle engagement."

"Oh." She gazed down at her handkerchief. His words brought a pang of memory, the image of him lying on the couch in his London home, his mouth pale, the lines beside it white with pain, trying gallantly to smile at her teasing. But she must not let that memory betray her into weakness. "Nevertheless, sir, we are different, both of us. Those two people who engaged themselves —no longer exist. Instead, here are two strangers, in an—awkward—situation."

She thought she had worded that quite beautifully and finally. She was outraged when he made a rude sound, like a schoolboy.

"Hah! Stupidity. We are the same people. And we are definitely engaged. I am sure that after we are married and better acquainted, Pamela, you will be able to conform more to the image I wish. You see, I am in Diplomatic now, and you will be expected—"

This was more than she could endure. She leaped up, quivering. "I—to conform—" she cried out. "How dare you! I—conform—when it is you who goes riding out in your phaeton with—with an Italian woman—with—" The words died at the blaze in his eyes.

"So that is the heart of the matter," he said slowly. "You are jealous of Signorina Lanza. She is a friend, a dear friend, and I admire and respect her family immensely. We fought together in several engagements—"

"Then pray consider this one more engagement, and conclude it with her!" she shot at him triumphantly. "For I shall not marry you! Never—*never!*" And she dashed from the room into the hallway.

Douglas was coming behind her. Adelaide stood at the foot of the stairway, her face ominous. Sir William was coming from the study.

Pamela felt like a trapped fox. "I shall never marry him, *never!*" she cried to them all, and turned and dashed through a drawing room, out to the terrace. She paused, then ran on, out through the gardens, to the fountain area and beyond to the woods.

She had never been so humiliated and ashamed and crushed. He thought she was jealous! He thought she would—*conform!* Be a meek English wife, while he carried on with other women as he chose! Well, she would not—never, never, *never!*

She sank down weeping into the tall grass beneath a comforting shade tree. She cried into her violet handkerchief until the tears of rage subsided. Then she sat, furiously, trying to plan, trying to think what to do.

"I say—Pamela? Mind if I sit down?" It was a rather meek, sweet voice. She glanced up, surprised to find Roger Saltash. Douglas's aide was usually near him. He was standing about twenty feet away, looking at her with grave worried brown eyes.

"I don't mind," she said. "Only don't try to persuade me to marry Douglas! I hate him!" She pulled up a clump of grass violently to show her intensity.

Roger came over and sat down beside her, and took one of her hands gently, almost reverently. "You should not be so upset, Pamela. You are one of the sweet people of the earth, one of the lovely ones. Everything ought to be smooth in your path, not difficult."

She thought he talked like a poet. She sniffed again and managed to smile at him. "Oh Roger, everyone pushes me," she said forlornly. "And Douglas—why, he likes that Beata. He doesn't really want to marry me, only he promised my parents—"

"I have had an idea," he said after a pause. "You know, I don't have money or anything, only my position. But if you would condescend to marry me, I should try awfully hard to make you happy. I love you, Pamela, I adore you."

She opened her wet violet eyes wide at him. "*Love* me? How can you?" she asked blankly.

He flushed. "I realize our positions are much—"

"No, no—I mean, how *can* you when you have known me so short a time?"

"Oh that; I loved you at first sight," he said gravely. He took her hand in both of his. "Will you marry me, Pamela?"

"Oh, I would like to." She really liked the way he talked, and this was a very romantic situation here in the woods, after her severe distress. "I should like to, Roger, really."

"Oh, good!" he said boyishly, smiling at her. He bent and kissed her cheek shyly. "I don't know what the circumstances are all about, but Douglas is a bit of a tyrant, isn't he? You would not be half appreciated! I shall do my best to care for you, dearest."

They talked, strolling happily back to the house, hand in hand. "We shall have to have an elopement," she said briskly. "Addy will never consent, after her grand plans! So we shall elope, and not a word to anyone, Roger!"

"I'm not afraid, now that you love me," he said.

She frowned. She had not said she loved him. Did it matter?

"*Here* you are at last," said Douglas's angry

voice. She started, and found him standing quite near them on the terrace, glaring at them. "Where the devil have you both been?"

"You shall not speak to my fiancée like that," said Roger firmly. "We are going to be married—"

"*Married!*" squeaked Adelaide behind Douglas. "Oh God, no!"

"I say there, she is engaged to Douglas," rumbled Sir William, coming out of the house to stand beside Adelaide. "Can't possibly, old chap. She is engaged—"

"Yes she is, no matter how badly she behaves," said Douglas furiously. "And this is all nonsense! I shall leave now. Come along, Saltash! I shall need you for a meeting. I have spent quite enough time here today! We have work to do!" And he turned about on his heel and marched away.

Pamela called after him childishly, in triumph, "But I am going to marry Roger! I told you—I will not marry you!"

He flung around, glaring at her for an ominous moment. "Nonsense!" he barked, and departed.

Roger tenderly kissed her hand and then her cheek. "I shall see you tomorrow, love. Be brave," he said cheerfully, and left her to face her sister.

CHAPTER FIVE

Adelaide was furious, though as usual she had good control of her temper. Nevertheless, Pamela was under a cloud of displeasure for the evening and next morning.

She retreated into the library and buried herself in the latest gazettes from Paris and London. She was reading, quite absorbed in the news and forgetful of her own problems, when the footman brought Douglas in to her.

She dropped the papers with a rustle, gazing up at him blankly. "Oh—you," she said rudely, with a frown.

"Good morning, Pamela," he said blandly. The footman bowed and left the room, closing the door after him. "Ah—I see you have the latest from London. May I?"

A little startled at his manner after yesterday, she handed the pages to him. He seated himself at the library table opposite her and began to read, frowning a little.

She went on with her paper in French, scanning it quickly until she reached the items she wanted. Then she was aware that he had lifted his head and was watching her.

"You read French fluently?" he asked politely. "I recall you were studying it under a tutor in London."

"Yes, I understand it rather well. I speak it with some accent yet," she replied, amazed at his calm manner. One would have thought they had never quarreled.

"And what other languages do you speak? Italian, I understand."

"I am just learning Italian. Signora Margotti is helping me. I can read and speak German and Latin—that is all."

"All?" A slight smile softened his hard face. "That is amazing. Few ladies care to trouble themselves with the study of languages. You shall help me immensely in the Diplomatic. A foreigner is always flattered with a Britisher who speaks his tongue."

She glanced down uneasily. He seemed to have

ignored the fact that she had broken her engagement to him and planned to marry Roger. "But I—" she began.

"And are you interested in reading the news in the gazettes? You have not turned to the fashion notes."

Her face lighted. She widened her violet eyes at him. "Oh, but I *am* interested! What will happen to poor Italy when Napoleon is defeated?"

"When? I wish I had your confidence! Yes, I think you are right, though. When Napoleon is defeated—we should be thinking more about that and making plans."

"Carlo told me that when Napoleon is defeated the Italians will be engaged in a life-and-death struggle to win their own future! He says that other nations, including Britain, will attempt to impose settlements, and the Italians are determined to finally choose their own future and not have it forced upon them."

"Carlo?" asked Douglas smoothly. "Do you still see him?"

She flushed. "I have not seen him since he left," she said honestly. "But we used to have long conversations. I—I really trust him, Douglas."

He frowned. "Have nothing to do with him," he said curtly. "I do not wish you involved in such matters. My mission here is delicate enough without having my fiancée involved with a questionable Italian spy! I wish you had confided in me, Pamela, instead of taking it into your own hands to help him."

She glared at him, her mouth tightening mutinously. "You seem to forget, sir, that I have broken our engagement! I mean to marry Roger!"

"Why? Because he is more docile, and you think you can handle him?" The smooth question came from smiling lips, but the eyes were challenging her.

"That was hatefully put, sir! I like Roger because he is gentle and kind. He likes me immensely!"

"That is no foundation for a marriage. Besides, it is out of the question. We are engaged, and our wedding plans are moving forward. But we were speaking of the plans for Italy—have you seen this item?"

He stood up and moved around the table with the pages in his large, tanned hand. He set them before her and bent over her shoulder as she read. She found herself curiously disturbed at his closeness, his red head near hers as they read the item in the London gazette. She found it hard to concentrate. She decided she was furiously angry at him, that was why.

She read it, they discussed it for a time, he pointed out another item in her French gazette, and they talked about it, becoming interested in their argument. They managed to argue without becoming angry at the matter, exchanging views in a lively fashion.

Presently the door opened and Adelaide came in, attractively dressed in a blue morning gown. "Oh, here you are. I am so sorry to be late, my lord! The household, you know," she said vaguely, beaming at them both.

Pamela read her devious sister. Adelaide had deliberately left them together to settle their differences. Ordinarily, she would not have left them unchaperoned.

Lord Douglas kissed her plump hand and told her she looked radiant, and then they seated themselves on the sofa. Pamela remained at the library table pretending to read further in the journals. Her sister kept glancing at her, then said mildly, "Do come over here and help us plan, love!"

Pamela said quietly, "There is nothing to plan, Addy. I have told you both, I am going to marry Roger. There is no hurry about our plans. We may return to England for the wedding!"

She did not know what demon made her say these things. She and Roger had discussed nothing.

"Now darling, don't be obstinate. Of *course* you are going to marry Douglas. It has been planned for years!"

"Too many years," said Pamela. "He no longer

wishes to marry me, and I never did wish to marry him!" She flung these words defiantly at the red-headed man, watching his green eyes narrow as the shot went home.

"Of course you do, you always adored Douglas," said her sister tactlessly.

Pamela flushed wildly and jumped to her feet. "I did not! Oh, that is a shocking lie, Addy! How can you say it? You know our parents planned it all. I had nothing to say about the matter! Well, I am of age now, and I tell you—"

"Adelaide, if you will leave us for a time, I would appreciate it," said Douglas coldly.

Adelaide got up at once. Douglas rose and bowed her out of the room before turning to Pamela.

When the door was shut, he said in a coldly controlled voice, "Pamela, if we were married, I should want to shake you or spank you! I am sure I shall give way to my feelings one day! You are a spoiled, troublesome brat, and you were even as a child! I do not know how I shall endure it, but I must! I promised!"

"Oh!" she gasped, outraged. "How dare you say such things! I will never marry you. If you attempt to strike me, I shall—I shall kick you!" she spat at him as he came closer.

His big hands closed over her slim shoulders. For a moment she thought he would carry out his threat. She began to struggle, seeing the warning in his green eyes. He caught her close to him and locked one arm about her to pull her against his hard body. She was tall, but not nearly so tall as he. She kicked at him, and her sharp toe in the soft slipper hit his shin.

"Ouch! You brat—" he said, and put his mouth down hard on hers. He held her motionless, one arm about her, one arm locked about her head, his hand holding her face up remorselessly to his.

She tried to kick him again. He locked his leg about hers deftly and she felt stifled as he kissed her again and again, his lips hotly, angrily on hers.

She felt such fury and welling emotion she quite choked with it. Her foot ached where she had kicked him; she thought she had hurt herself more than him! Was it symbolic that when she tried to hurt him she only succeeded in hurting herself?

She tried to turn her head away from his hard lips. She could not—she was locked tight. He held her head firmly and pressed his lips again to hers. She thought she read contempt and condescension in that kiss, as though she were really a child, a silly chit he could quell with a punishing series of kisses.

He took her breath away and she could not struggle. She went limp as the kiss went on and on. Emotions were flashing through her whole body, hot feelings that she dimly identified as fury, or—or something else.

"Oh—oh—*hateful*—" she managed to sputter, as his head lifted for a moment. She glared at him. He was smiling! "Brute! Devil!" She tried to strike him, but her arms were locked to her sides.

He released her and stepped back so swiftly she could not strike at him. She was glaring at him, her eyes sparkling with tears of rage at her helplessness.

"You are but a child, I keep forgetting," he said softly. "You have much to learn—about life, and kisses—" He was looking at her soft, bruised mouth.

"Not from you!" she cried out, rubbing her mouth furiously with her hand. "Never touch me again—*never!* I hate you! You are a bully—you care nothing for me! I will never marry you!"

He bowed courteously, mockingly. "Next month, my love. I look forward to our—next encounter!" And he had the gall to laugh as he left her!

She was raging when Adelaide returned. Her sister's smile vanished as she read Pamela's true fury. "Oh dear, what now?" sighed the plump matron. "Really, Pamela, can you not control your temper? He is red-haired—you must learn to speak mildly, or you will enrage him!"

"He enrages *me!*" cried the bedeviled girl. "Oh Addy, don't you see, he is such a brute and a bully! I cannot marry him. Do you want me to live in misery?"

"No, I shall expect you to conform to his desires and to be more meek, my dearest," said her sister, more sternly than usual. "Indeed, you are trying him sorely. I shall expect him to fly off if you continue!"

"That is exactly what I want him to do!"

"Nonsense, absurd!" said Adelaide, and left her.

Pamela raged out into the garden and paced about among the flowers until she felt more calm. He was indeed a bully. She rubbed her lips fiercely again and again, but they still stung from his kisses. She went to luncheon when called, but could eat little, she was so angry. Adelaide, for once, would not take her side in the matter. Sir William was preoccupied with some other matter, and Adelaide silently warned Pamela not to speak to him about her troubles.

About mid-afternoon, the footman informed her that Sir Roger Saltash wished to see her in the drawing room. Pamela flew down to him eagerly. He was her one means of escape. She would plan their elopement at once. *That* would show his lordship!

Roger was pale, drawn, and serious. He greeted her with a formal bow and kissed her hand gently before putting it down.

"Oh Roger, have you been making our plans?" she asked eagerly. She went over and shut the door firmly, regardless of convention, and returned to him. She drew him down on the sofa beside her, and studied his face.

"Pamela, how can I say this? Douglas has been my friend, the friend of my family for years. When he came to me this noon, and said to me, you must speak to Pamela, and convince her you will not marry her—what could I say? What else could I do? He has been my best friend, more than an employer—"

"Oh, Roger!" she said reproachfully, her heart sinking. "You—I thought you would help me—"

"I want to help you, but I cannot do this. Pamela, forgive me, but I must retract my offer. I cannot break the marriage plans of my best friend, the kindest man I have ever known, who has helped me over and over again."

He was serious, he meant it. Pamela was furious all over again. That Douglas—he meant to have his own way all the time.

"But you could marry me quickly, we could elope," she said, coaxingly, taking his hand and playing with it teasingly. "Roger, he would forgive you and so would my sister, once the deed was done! Come along, be sporting about it! Let's elope—"

He was silent, staring into space for a time, his

71

lips compressed. He was more serious than she had ever known him to be, and a sigh escaped her.

"Pamela, I know what the problem is," he said finally. "The Signorina Lanza—you are jealous of her, are you not? Well, you must not be. For Douglas is a man of honor, I assure you. She is a beautiful, enticing woman, but he is not engaged to her, as he is to you. He will forget her in time, and turn only to you, I assure you!"

She stiffened haughtily, her face turning scarlet. "She is not the reason," she began hotly. "There are many reasons—he is not only a rake and libertine, he is a bully and means to dominate me—"

"So does any true man who marries," said Roger simply. "You must expect that, Pamela. Marriages today are like that. Of course, subtly you may influence him to do as you wish, after your marriage. But you know that." He smiled, and patted her hand in friendly fashion. "And you are so beautiful that he will give you your head many a time, I warrant!"

"And he will continue to have his—his mistresses! I warrant you that!" she said recklessly, tears gathering in her violet eyes. She had never felt so helpless. Even Roger, gentle and kindly as he was, would not aid her.

"Probably so," said Roger simply. "I am speaking frankly to you, Pamela, because I admire you.

Only the truth will do for you, I can see that. Yes, he is a rake and a libertine, and you cannot expect for him to be faithful to you. But he will respect you and keep his marriage vows. And he will be good to the children! You must learn to ignore the other side of him, to turn the head, so to speak."

"A dreadful life!" she whispered half to herself, her head bent. Now that Roger had put her doubts into words, they seemed more real and frightening. She did not want the usual British society marriage where the husband went his way—to Vauxhall Gardens with his latest doxy—and the wife drove past in her carriage with her head politely averted. Where the husband nodded at the opera, and his wife sat close to her own lover in full view of the curious public. Where only a mutual interest in the children, the estate, the fortune, kept them from living apart—coldly and with no love between them.

In all her years of being engaged to Douglas, she had not dreamed he would be like this. She had known he was extremely busy, first with the battles on the Peninsula, later in other battles in Parliament and on the Continent in the Diplomatic. But to know that all these years there had been a succession of mistresses—attractive, drawing him, keeping his attention fixed for a time until he wearied of one and took another—

She shuddered convulsively and Roger patted her hand once more, his face very anxious, his brown eyes like a spaniel's.

"I am sorry, my dear," he said, and took his departure, leaving her to gaze into space, seeing a very dreary future ahead. She had expected to quarrel with Douglas, but not—not to have the coldness between them, to have mistresses between them, to know he had no true affection or regard for her. A marriage arranged and drawn up by contract—nothing of love or warmth.

Oh, she could not endure that. She could not. What way to turn, what could she do?

Signora Margotti came to her. "Did you forget, my lady, that you ordered the carriage for four o'clock?" she asked in Italian. Her keen eyes studied Pamela's white face with sympathy and compassion. "Come, let us go out into the streets of Rome, my lady. They will help you forget all!"

"Yes, yes, to forget," whispered Pamela, and she got up, her hand to her face. The Signora had brought her cloak and sketching materials.

They drove down into the artists' quarter of Rome. Pamela remembered that Douglas had expressed his strong wish that she should not do so. It was a small gesture of defiance, but it made her feel a little better.

They alighted at a favorite café and she set out her sketching materials. The artists were sketching, laughing, talking, and drinking endless cups of coffee. The pencil remained motionless in her languid hand, her gaze fixed in space. The life ahead of her stretched out in a dreary, frightening mist.

"Miss—my lady—" the whisper finally penetrated the haze about her.

She turned her head slowly.

"No, do not look toward me! It is I, Carlo—I am sitting at the table behind you, my lady. Oh, how good to see you. I have waited two days to see you."

"You are—all right?" she whispered. Signora Margotti sat rigidly, grandly staring ahead of her, though she also must have heard the whispering.

"I—I am well, thank you. I must—hide out, and it is difficult. I have—few friends."

There was no time for polite conversation, going gradually to the matter. "Carlo, tell me quickly, honestly. Do you need money? Tell me—"

"Ah—signorina, I—I am hungry," the whisper ended in a sigh of despair.

Slowly she opened her purse, as though absently groping in it. She took out a handkerchief. The Signora leaned over, took a napkin from the table instead, a snowy white napkin the café owner had brought to the grand lady who came to sketch.

"In here, my lady," whispered the Signora.

Pamela took out all the money she had with her, the coins and bills, and piled it into the napkin. The signora added some coins she had, and wrapped up the napkin carefully.

"I will order more coffee, my lady," said Signora Margotti in a louder tone. She rose grandly to her full five feet, and snowy head high, went past Carlo's table to the waiter.

Pamela waited stiffly, her back to Carlo, her mouth set, her teeth clenched. The Signora returned without the napkin.

The waiter came, they ordered more coffee and cakes, and ate slowly. When the area was clear again, Pamela whispered, "I will bring more money tomorrow, Carlo."

"Be careful. God bless you," he murmured.

A few minutes later, the Signora murmured, "He has departed. No one noticed him, or paid attention."

"Thank Heaven," Pamela murmured. "How— how did he look?"

"Weary, unshaved, gallant. He is a man of much courage," whispered the Signora. Pamela glanced toward her. The Signora had sparkling bright eyes, her mouth curved in a smile.

"And I shall earn my fiancé's fury if he learns of this," said Pamela, not without satisfaction. "But he shall not learn of it from me! Tomorrow again, Signora, we shall come to sketch!"

"*Brava*, you have much courage also, my lady! Tonight, we shall read again in the history book that *he* recommended. You shall learn more of the bloody, violent, *glorious* history of our Italia!"

Pamela felt much more satisfied and much happier as they finally left in the late afternoon. The evening blue was just beginning to fill the square, and the sky was turning russet and orange in the west. Rome seemed filled with a glitter and a glamour she had never known.

Ah, her life should be more exciting also, she resolved! Life was too fascinating to be thrown away in a dull marriage to a man who spent most of his spare time with his mistresses! She would find a way to attack this problem—with courage, as the Italians said. Courage, patience! She would win!

CHAPTER SIX

The next morning, Pamela asked her brother-in-law's secretary to obtain more Italian money for her. The Italian, accustomed to the eccentricities of the British, obtained the money for her, and brought it to her sitting room in the early afternoon.

She at once planned with Signora Margotti to go out sketching at the cafés.

When informed they were going out, Adelaide said, "But love, tonight is the Grand Ball. Lord Douglas calls for us at seven, you know. You won't be late, will you, dearest, and make him angry?"

Pamela hesitated. She would love to be so late that she would infuriate him.

"And your new adorable ball gown is all ready," sighed Adelaide.

Pamela though of the swirling blue green gown caught up with tiny golden thistles, her new lord's emblem. No, it was really too pretty a gown to waste! "I'll be back in good time, Addy, I promise!"

She and the Signora went out sketching, ended up at the same café, and presently Carlo's whisper came from behind her. Again, they wrapped the money in a table napkin, and Signora Margotti delivered it inconspicuously.

"Where are you going, what will you do, Carlo?" whispered Pamela.

"I must not tell you. But you will see me again. Your generous help will enable me to continue the work. How grateful I am, my lady, and how grateful Italy would be if she but knew!"

They talked only a little, for fear of being overheard. She told him of the book she was reading with Signora Margotti's assistance, he recommended yet another, and told her a new journal to read. Then he left, as swiftly and silently as he had come.

"A very gallant man," she said, in a low tone to her companion.

"Ah yes, if Italia had more of his caliber—!" and the woman's eyes shone again with fervor.

She returned to the villa in good time to change into the new ball gown. It was quite the most attractive one she owned, she thought with pride, as she turned about again and again before the full-length mirrors in her dressing room. The unusual sea green, an odd, vivid blue green, was wrought in a gauze so fine that it floated in the palm, yet so full were the skirts that they spread out about her long slim legs like waves.

The bodice was tight, rather low about her cream-colored shoulders and bosom. The sleeves were only thin gauze. The bodice and the skirts were pricked about with tiny golden thistles deftly sewn so that they sparkled when caught by the lights. Fanny set the deep blue cloak over her shoulders, and she was ready.

She descended the wide stairs and was a little disconcerted to find her lord waiting at the bottom of the stairs, staring up at her. He, too, was in blue green, a formal garb with velvet jacket and golden decorations, among which was a golden thistle.

He took her hand, and helped her down the last two steps. He raised her hand slowly to his lips, still gazing down at her from his lean height. His red hair seemed to flame in the light of the candles.

"You honor me and my house by wearing my colors, Pamela," he said formally.

She thought of some flippant remarks, some cutting ones, and discarded them as unworthy.

"Thank you—Douglas," she said. "I am glad you are pleased."

Helping Carlo today had soothed her hurt vanity, made her feel more useful, not just an object. Now she was able to smile up at her fiancé, and his green eyes flickered.

The dinner was to begin promptly. Douglas escorted Pamela and her chaperon out to the carriage, handed them in, and they saw Adelaide and Sir William following in the next carriage. Douglas was most solicitious of her comfort, assuring himself the cloak was sufficiently warm, the rug over her knees, yet not mussing the fragile gown.

Then he leaned back and began chatting about the news of the day. He spoke in Italian and she answered, timidly at first, then with more confidence.

He paused to compliment her once. "You will please the host tonight, he speaks no English. I am most gratified that you have taken the trouble to learn Italian."

She was pleased, but tried to hide it and the fluttering of her heart. He sounded almost like the boy she had known, complimenting her on the way she rode her horse.

"You must thank the patience of Signora Margotti. She has been most good at helping me," she said lightly.

Douglas smiled at the bright-eyed chaperon and thanked her. The smile seemed to light his face and lighten his manner.

They arrived at the villa of their host all too soon. It was really the first time Pamela had felt comfortable in the presence of her fiancé in the past month. She glanced about warily to see if the Lanza family was there, and experienced a quick lightness when she realized they were not.

She had the first dance with Douglas. She was surprised when he swung her out into the dance, for he still limped from his Peninsular war wound. But he was light on his feet and had a natural grace and rhythm.

She managed to relax in his arms and yield herself to the movements. Her eyes were starry when the music ended. "Oh, I did enjoy that," she said involuntarily.

He smiled down at her, his green eyes gentle for once. "Did you? We must dance more often. We cannot quarrel while we are moving in rhythm!"

Then before she could catch him up or berate him, he laughed, and smoothly introduced her to their host who claimed a dance. Pamela charmed the man with her Italian and her compliments to Rome, and he returned every compliment with a fulsome one to her beauty, her English complexion, her fairness. He gave her up very reluctantly at the end of the dance.

She was scarcely off the dance floor the entire evening. She danced several times with Douglas, and he introduced her generously to several friends, who claimed dances, and complimented her.

"One would think they had never seen a blond," she told Douglas and Adelaide rather breathlessly after one dance. "They cannot stop saying how blond I am!"

"The Italians are enchanted with blonds, they see so few. I can understand I must guard my fiancée even more closely," said Douglas, a naughty twinkle in his eyes.

She dared to make a quick face at him, her mouth puckering in a daring taunt. His eyes darkened warningly. Adelaide said, "Pamela, dearest," weakly.

"She does hate to be guarded, doesn't she?" Douglas commented.

Adelaide gave a deep, heartful sigh, and the other two laughed in concert.

"Do not be worried, my dear sister," said Douglas to Adelaide. "I shall soon take this little worry off your hands, and have a care myself! You have put up with much through the years. I must compliment you on the patience and fortitude you have exhibited!"

"Oh really, Douglas!" Pamela began to flare up. He grinned at her, caught her by her waist, and swung her recklessly into the dance. "Really, you are—abominable!"

"I enjoy teasing you, as I used to," he said, and smiled down at her. "You flare up so fast. I enjoy seeing your blue eyes sparkle with fury— only they are violet, are they not? Let me see them?"

She glared up at him.

"Yes, violet," he said coolly, "like an English violet. As a child, your temper tantrums amused me mightily. Like a little fairy imp enraged by mortals! You have not changed much."

She was silent in sheer surprise. A fairy imp? Was that what he had thought? She had thought him a godlike creature, far above her, in their youth. She had adored him, followed him, allowed herself to be teased, dared to ride a stallion he said she could. When they had become engaged, she had thought all her dreams had come true. Only—only now—he was older, and a stranger.

Yet *not* a stranger. His red head was familiar to her, his green eyes, his imperious face, his height, his Scottish burr as he murmured in her ear teasingly. How handsome he appeared in his greenish blue Scottish uniform with the gold on it. His golden thistle—she glanced at it as he held her a little way from him in the dance. Hers was like it, only much smaller, and even now it pricked her through the thin gauze, as it was pinned to her underbodice.

Maybe—maybe it would not be so bad after all, she thought, as he whirled her about. Beata Lanza was not here tonight and Douglas was paying Pamela marked attention. Perhaps he was through with Beata, and their marriage might have some chance of happiness.

Then she thought of Roger's words, about his many mistresses, the fact that he was a rake and a libertine, and she sobered again.

"You look so serious." His lips brushed her ear as he whispered, and an involuntary thrill shot through her. "Smile for me! Smile—"

She glanced up at him shyly. He was smiling down at her, his green eyes flashing. She finally returned his smile.

"There—that's my lovely," he said, and pressed her close quickly as the dance ended.

She felt in a daze. Had he changed, or had she? She felt rather—enchanted. He could be so charming and so sweet when he wanted to. She had not seen this side of him for a long time, she thought, not since he was a young man and she a girl, just engaged to him.

As she danced with another man, automatically smiling at his compliments, she kept thinking of Douglas. Yes, he did have charm, grace, poise. He was quite capable of making a girl fall madly in love with him. Beata Lanza was obviously enamoured of him, and her father did nothing to stop their relationship—whatever it was. And she had thought Italian girls were so sheltered! But Beata and Douglas had been driving about in Rome without a chaperon!

Douglas took her in to supper, filled her plate, and brought her glasses of the sparkling white Italian wine she enjoyed. He stayed devotedly at her side—it *must* look like devotion, she decided drily. He bent to her, listened to her every remark, studied her with his bright green eyes keenly.

They did not try to speak of politics, there were too many varied factions present in the neutral ground of their wealthy host. The British were in a precarious position in Italy, Douglas had warned Pamela and her relatives. The British blockade of ports, the Continental blockades, interference with shipping and trade, the position of Napoleon following his defeats in Russia—all were making everyone very uneasy.

Douglas informed her of the identity of several important personages, saw that she was introduced to many, saw that every dance she wanted to dance was taken care of, guarded her fragile gown—in short, she seemed to be the very suitor any girl would wish for.

Even her chaperon was cared for. Douglas went over to her several times to make sure she was comfortable and had supper and wines. Signora Margotti was with several friends, and her bright eyes sparkled as she talked animatedly with them.

On the way home, she confided that she had had a delicious time.

"Is that right, *delicious?*"

Pamela giggled out loud. "Yes, it was delicious, you are quite right, Signora?" she said.

Douglas smiled across the carriage at her. They brushed knees at times, and she could feel her gauze skirts move as his legs stretched to find room. He was so very tall, so long and lean.

She thought of him riding horseback across the Scottish hills, herself chasing along on her black stallion, calling to him, "I can catch up, I can, just wait up a little bit, Douglas!" and his laughter ringing out as he pulled up a bit to let her catch him.

She smiled involuntarily at the memory, gazing out dreamily into the purple Roman night. What a sense of history, of memories running together, one had in Rome. It might be any period, from the very earliest of the primitive men, or that of Julius Caesar, of the bloody times of the Vandal hordes sweeping across Italy, or the grandeur of the Renaissance.

"What are you thinking, Pamela?" asked Douglas, not in a demanding way, but as though he cared.

"Oh—of Rome. Of its history," she said dreamily. "All those who have come and gone—the color, the pagentry, the beauty—"

"None so beautiful as you this evening," he said quietly. "Did I tell you how lovely you are? Your beautiful English face, and that sea green color of your gown, your grace—"

"Truly an English rose," said Signora Margotti proudly.

"No, an English violet," he said, smiling.

She was numb with his compliments. Was he planning a campaign to conquer her reluctance to the marriage? His methods were very overwhelming, she admitted ruefully. She felt much more reconciled to the wedding tonight.

They arrived home and Douglas escorted them inside. Adelaide followed them into the hallway, yawning frankly. "Laws, am I weary! My feet— I must have danced half the dances tonight!"

"With your permission, I should like to bid Pamela goodnight in the drawing room," said Douglas, and without waiting, he drew her into the dimly lit room.

"Oh yes, of course," Adelaide's voice followed them. "My lands, I am weary—it is to bed with me!"

Pamela scarcely heard her. Douglas, in the privacy of the room, had drawn her abruptly into his arms. But tonight he was not rough and angry. He held her gently, though firmly.

"You—should—not—" she said in a daze, turning her head. His hand touched her cheek and turned her face so it was just under his. His head bent.

She could not see his face or his eyes, which reflected his moods. There was only his mouth, claiming hers, softly at first. Then more firmly, hotly, flaming against hers.

She stood there, unable to fight him, though tonight his arms were not cruel and cordlike. He was gentle, and she could not resist him.

His flame lit hers. Her head was bent back against his arm, and her lips began to respond to his. She kissed shyly at first, then more ardently as fire built up in her. She felt drawn taut, pressing herself urgently against his body as his arm drew her closer to him. Her gauze skirts were quite crushed against his uniform. She felt limp, unable to fight, yet so hot and emotional that she felt quite dazed.

Slowly, he let her go. She could scarcely stand. He tucked her hand into his arm, and drew her to the door.

"See me to the terrace," he said softly into her ear. She went with him like a puppet, she thought, rather angry at her weakness.

At the front entrance, he let go of her arm and raised her hand to his lips. She felt his lips burning against her palm.

"Till tomorrow morning, Pamela. I shall come about ten o'clock. Good night, my lovely!"

And he was gone. She went back inside and up the stairs, dreamily. Douglas, she thought—oh, you man of many moods! What can I believe of you?

CHAPTER SEVEN

Pamela slept deeply, dreaming about Douglas, a misty figure on a high black stallion. His red hair flamed against a Scottish grey sky, he was riding, riding, where? Away from her?

She could not catch him, she called out, "Wait for me, oh, wait for me, I love you—I love—"

When she wakened, she wondered at herself. She did not love him, of course not! Why had she dreamed that?

She rose late, sleepy-eyed. Fanny asked about the ball and Pamela satisfied her that her mistress had been very popular, that her dress had been much complimented.

Mindful that Douglas was coming again that

morning, she put on a favorite blue muslin, demure and feminine. Perhaps she could manage not to lose her temper with him today!

When she went downstairs, it was to find him already in the library, absorbed in gazettes. He set them aside promptly as she entered, smiling at her gently.

"You are quite bright, Pamela, after such a late evening! That bodes well for our future."

She grimaced, caught his warning eyes, then laughed, her face flushed pink. "And you—are you good-tempered every morning?" she asked audaciously.

"That is something you must decide for yourself," he said, with a curious smile. Her flush deepened, and she turned hastily to the gazettes.

"What is the news this morning?" She turned over a sheet, not seeing it clearly.

They were called to breakfast, chatted of nothing but the ball, and returned to the library.

"Now, I believe there is some discussion we need to have," said Douglas. He pulled out a sheet of paper on which were notes in his neat handwriting. "I had consulted your sister on several matters about the wedding. But about the honeymoon, I thought we would proceed to a villa in Florence I have rented. Will that please you?"

"Oh, I don't know—" she said vaguely. She had been curious to see the beauties of Florence, but with him—and on a honeymoon? She did not wish to marry, she kept telling herself.

"The journey is long and tiring. I thought we might break it at the villas of friends along the way. The visiting will be kept to an informal pace. Would you like to do this?"

She turned on him impatiently, feeling hot and confused. "Oh Douglas, I do not want—" she began rashly, and was warned by the flare of warning in his green eyes. "I—I don't want to discuss details this—this morning," she ended weakly. Her hand flipped over the pages of a gazette from Paris. "What—what do you think will happen to Italy if Murat fails?"

He sighed a little, but sat down beside her on the couch and answered her questions patiently. They had quite a little discussion about politics and he enlightened her on the background of the news. He talked about the future of the Polish state and what might happen to several of the smaller German states. She found it much more fascinating than details of her wedding!

She kept him talking about it for a time, before he finally returned to the subject of their marriage. He got out the paper again and asked questions.

She answered vaguely again.

"Well, if it doesn't matter to you," he said with a slight frown, setting the paper in his pocket again, "then I shall proceed to make our plans. You *do* wish to visit Florence, do you not? I recall one evening we spoke of Florence, and you expressed a wish to see the art objects there. They are quite worth your time, I assure you."

"Yes, I thought Signora Margotti could go with me if—if you are absorbed in—business," she ended weakly.

He looked thoughtful. "I had not thought to take your chaperon on our wedding journey," he finally commented drily, looking down at her as she averted her face.

"Oh, I—I thought you might be quite busy, with the—the Diplomatic," she said bravely. "Roger Saltash is accompanying us, isn't he?"

"Yes, he is my aide. There might be matters arising—but of course you can speak Italian to Signora Margotti, and practice that. I do not wish you going out sketching alone, however," he added dogmatically, she thought.

Her mouth tightened obstinately. He was not going to cut off all her pleasures after her marriage—if she married him!

"I wanted to speak quite frankly with you, Douglas," she said, after a pause. "About our marriage. I do wish to terminate our engagement! Won't you consider my arguments, and think seriously—"

"Pamela, you really try my patience," he said

roughly, and stood up to stride about the room. She watched him out of the corners of her eyes. The room was large, but he dominated it with his height and strength. She noticed he limped more than usual today. Was he tired from dancing? She felt anxious about that.

"Does your leg hurt?" she blurted out.

"My what?"

He turned to her in amazement, staring down at her.

She clasped her hands together in her lap, and returned his stare, though she was flushing. "Your limp—I mean—from the wound."

"Oh. Yes, slightly. From the dancing last night, I expect. But I enjoyed it. And you?" He was almost smiling, his mouth relaxed.

"Yes, but I should not if it pains you afterwards, Douglas. Really, you ought to take more care!"

"Does it disgust you?" he asked.

"Disgust?" She gasped. "Oh no, not that—why, you earned that—the Peninsular Wars—" she was stammering, unable to express her pride and her concern for him without betraying more feeling than she wished.

He was still gazing at her keenly, a shadow flickering in his eyes. He turned away abruptly, and she was distressed. Did he think she cared that way, that she should be repelled by his wound? She was proud of him, she could not express how proud and concerned she felt. Her hands twisted tightly together.

He walked over to the window and gazed out at the gardens for a short time before returning to her. "Your sister has been good enough to invite me for luncheon. Then we go on to the reception this afternoon, you recall," he said formally.

"Yes, I remember." Her voice was stifled. She was still upset that he thought her so flighty as to be distressed for herself over his wound. What did he really think of her?

They were called for luncheon, and the conversation became general. Adelaide, after a keen look at their two faces, took up the burden of supplying topics that were innocuous. Poor Adelaide, thought her sister, ironically. She would be so relieved when they were married at last—*if* they did marry!

They went on to the reception, a birthday party for an elderly Italian gentleman—an excuse to bring together two rival political factions, Douglas had explained to her. Pamela would have been keenly amused and diverted by the charged situation had not Beata Lanza and her family attended. As soon as she saw them, she went stiff.

The Italian woman was elaborately attired in a dazzling red chiffon with black embroidery. Her black hair was sleekly upswept, her black eyes were soft as the wing of a bird. Her mouth was overly large, red as her gown from artificial coloring. Pamela felt pale and faded beside her.

The English girl sat on a blue sofa, with her blue brocade dress seeming to melt into the wallpaper behind her. The late October day was cool and gray with rain. She wished she were anywhere in the world but here.

Douglas seemed to have turned from her completely. He hung over Beata Lanza. Even Adelaide looked disapproving as Douglas laughed down at the Italian beauty, brought her cups of tea and small plates of cakes, and introduced her to all his friends. One would have thought *she* was his fiancée rather than the pale English blond...!

Their hostess took Pamela and Adelaide upstairs to her own sitting rooms for half an hour, as she had promised to discuss wedding customs in Italy and recommend a housekeeper for Pamela. The one in Douglas's villa was planning to leave to care for an ailing daughter. They had a nice pleasant chat, while all the time, Pamela was thinking about Douglas downstairs with Beata.

"How can I marry him? How can I possibly marry him?" she thought again and again, even while her lips smiled and her mouth uttered conventional phrases.

"I understand you have been studying our language," her hostess was saying, turning to Pamela again. "How charming and delightfully kind of you! The British do not often concern themselves with such matters; I understand they are quite busy. But for you to learn Italian, and your fiancé speaks it as a native Tuscan, I assure you—"

"Tuscan?" murmured Adelaide.

"One from around Florence, I believe," said Pamela rather diffidently, and was rewarded with a beaming smile from the Italian princess.

"You are correct. And Tuscan is quite the best spoken Italian! I am pleased that your accent is Tuscan. Your Signora Margotti speaks it fluently, and I applaud your wisdom in choosing her as your tutor."

"A most intelligent woman," said Pamela. "I am enjoying her companionship immensely. She has taught me more than language, I assure you. Much of my knowledge of Italian history comes from her."

"I cannot express to you how pleased I am that a future Diplomatic wife chooses to interest herself in learning our history also! This argues well for our future, and may I say for your own, and your husband's? Already we are looking forward to having you in our circles. I can only hope that my lord Kinnair plans to remain in Italy. We sorely need men of his caliber!"

Pamela smiled and murmured something to the

effect that she was flattered. She had much food for thought as the hostess escorted them downstairs again. Adelaide had also entertained such thoughts, for she spoke in a murmur when they were briefly alone.

"I *thought* she asked us upstairs for a purpose. She was sounding you out, dearest! You have passed the examination of her making, I assure you! Congratulations, love. She will send about the word that Douglas Kinnair, Earl of Fitzroy, has a wife to contend with! She was mightily pleased, and she has some say in the Italian Diplomatic!"

Pamela's momentary pleasure was soon gone, however, for when they returned to the drawing room, it was to find Douglas bending over Beata as she played the piano in one corner. They were quite alone, a pretty little scene that caught her eye at once and she went cold.

Even her hands seemed frozen as she seated herself on a sofa next to Adelaide and accepted yet another cup of tea. Their hostess glanced several times at Beata and Douglas, and her lips were a thin line. Elderly Joachim Lanza, in his wheelchair, was turned so as to observe them, and he seemed rather distressed.

Finally he wheeled himself over near Pamela, and plied her with gentle, indirect questions. "You have known my lord long?"

"All our lives, sir," she replied colorlessly.

"You were brought up together?"

"Yes, sir. That is, his home in Scotland was quite near mine in Northern England. Our parents were friends, and visited often. He was some years older, however."

"Ah yes, that is good. The older, wise counselor to his wife," he said with a smile, glancing again uneasily at his vivacious daughter. She had paused in her playing and was laughing up at Douglas. "My daughter is somewhat spoiled, I fear. She is my own daughter, my comfort, my only girl-child. How devoted she always has been—"

"That must have been a comfort to you," said Adelaide vaguely, as Pamela did not answer.

The afternoon droned on and on. If this was a sample of what she might expect as a wife—no, thank you very much, Pamela told his back silently. She was too spirited a woman to put up with that! He must find himself a little mouse for a wife!

And I bet his mouse won't speak Italian, or care about Italian history, either, she added spitefully.

Why not marry Beata, she asked him later, silently, in the carriage, and wished she dare suggest it out loud. But his eyes were as cold as her heart, and his mouth was a mocking cynical twist.

When they entered the villa, Pamela wanted nothing so much as to retreat to her room, but she was too proud to run. Douglas followed her into the library, and she turned to stand stiffly and wait for what he would say.

"I shall be out of town for two days, Pamela. I shall not see you tomorrow or the next day," he said quietly.

"I shall manage to endure it, sir," she said bitingly.

His eyes narrowed dangerously. After a pause, he said, "The plans are underway and there should be no questions. If anything comes up, Roger Saltash will be available for consultation."

"Since I have your permission, I shall feel free to—call upon his advice and services, sir!"

Now his green eyes flared. "I do not care for a sarcastic female, I should inform you! If you wish to punish me for something, or to question my activities, feel free to do so! But be honest and straightforward about it! I despise deviousness!"

If she complained about his behavior toward Beata, he would call her jealous. She was silent, standing stiffly before him.

"This afternoon was quite successful," he said more quietly. "You made a good impression on the princess. And the Lanza family is more reconciled to them, and to you. Old Joachim Lanza admires you, and so informed me of his hopes for our happy marriage."

"Indeed," she said frigidly. "He—seems kind. Though foolish."

"Foolish! He is a very intelligent man! A gallant

soldier, and so were his sons! His daughter has his own courage! What malice do you mean?" Now he was angry, and she turned colder.

She shrugged, and turned away. "I think you would do well to marry your Beata, and forget about your promises to my parents," she said with cold precision. "I am sure your friend Joachim Lanza would be most gracious about welcoming you into the family."

"Still harping on that theme?" he blazed. He caught at her shoulders violently, and pulled her back to stand before him. "I am tired of your remarks! And we are engaged to be married! I promised your parents, and I do not break my word. You would do well to remember I always keep my word! And I swear—I swear I shall punish you if you continue to provoke me!"

"I believe you," she said ironically, and tried to pull away. As though the effort enraged him further, he yanked her abruptly to him. She pushed him away as his mouth came down toward hers. She turned her head back and forth, her blond hair swinging in its loose arrangement as she tried to evade him.

His hands slid from her shoulders to her back. He pulled her hard toward his body and held her tightly. His rough cheek pressed against her smooth silken one, he held her hard and forced a kiss on her mouth.

She felt outraged, so hot with fury she wanted to slap him. He had ignored her, paid marked attention to Beata Lanza all the afternoon, now he would kiss her! No, he would not! She would fight him—and she tried. She struggled, kicked, wrestled futilely against his iron-muscled grip, until panting and out of breath, she was forced to submit. He pulled her closer, pressed his mouth hard to hers, again and again.

It was useless to struggle against him, he was too tough for her. She was forced to stand still, to submit as his lips clung to hers warmly. She would not respond.

He was trying to humiliate her, she thought. He was trying to prove he could master her. Well, he could with brute strength, but no other way. She would not give in with her mind or her soul.

She turned her face away as his kisses insisted. His mouth traveled slowly over her flushed cheek, down to her throat, above the blue muslin. She felt as though he burned her, and his arms were bruising.

He finally let her go. "A cold bride, that is all I need!" he said furiously, his eyes ranging contemptuously over her stiff body in the blue gown. His hand lingered on her blond hair, then fell to his side. "I shall see you when I return, and if you say one word, one damn word about not marrying me—I shall beat you!"

With that he left her. A fine farewell, she thought. A typical gesture, no doubt! Unable to face Adelaide, she ran up to her own room, and slammed the door hard.

CHAPTER EIGHT

Pamela was furious with herself for missing Douglas those two days. She moped about the house, quarreled with Adelaide until her patient sister retired in tears to her own sitting room, went out sketching into the forbidden streets of Rome, and stamped her foot at the dressmaker who was trying to fit her wedding dress.

She did not want to get married. Couldn't anyone understand and sympathize with that? Even Roger reprimanded her gently one evening when he came to dinner with some instructions from Douglas.

"Indeed, I fear you are not conducting yourself as a lady," he said rather primly.

She gave him a furious glance. "Because I don't

want to marry someone in love with another fe-male?" she asked. Fortunately, they were alone in a corner of the drawing room.

He looked rather scared. "Pamela, please—do not say that! I am sure his sentiments are toward you—all the proper feelings—" he said weakly.

She grimaced angrily, then caught Adelaide's anxious eye. If only there were some way of get-ting out of this hated wedding! She had thought and thought, but nothing would work. If this were England, she might escape to the country, put him off, delay. But she had no friends here who would shelter her, and Adelaide was set upon the wed-ding. Her usually gentle sister was quite firm and hard now, resisting all Pamela's pressures.

She must reconcile herself to a loveless marriage, and how stinging and cruel it would be!

Douglas returned and called upon her formally one rainy afternoon. The drawing room was cold and she felt chilled through. His manner was as cold as the draughts that blew the heavy drapes in the French windows.

And it was only a few days until their wedding day.

The day itself dawned cold and rainy. "Oh, if we might be in London, it might be shining, though it be November," sighed Fanny, as she dressed her mistress.

"I doubt it. It would probably be raining there

also," said Pamela. The skies wept for her, though her sister would not! Adelaide insisted on regarding it as a joyous occasion.

Pamela had breakfast in her room, her last free morning, she thought bitterly. She would continue to fight to be free. After all, there were some divorces now, the courts were allowing them. If Douglas and she could not endure one another, there was that remedy available.

"Finish your tea, duck," sighed Fanny.

"That is all I want," and Pamela pushed the tray from her.

"You are so white. I'll put a bit of coloring on your cheeks." And the maid produced the rouge and powders.

She had not slept well. Mindful of the long journey of four days, with visits at three villas, she had hoped for some rest, but it had not come. She felt weary and cross when she was finally dressed and ready.

Adelaide swept in, radiant and plump and ruddy-complexioned in her pale blue gown with a little train. She gazed in admiration at her sister.

"Oh, dearest, you are so beautiful, so—so like a bride!"

Pamela made a face at herself in the mirror, sullenly. The ivory white satin and the shimmering Brussels lace set off her blond beauty. Fanny had fastened her hair up in soft curls and waves and set the veil about it. The gown was demure, high to the throat, yet so tightly designed that her soft round bust and small waist were set off to perfection.

Her dress for the wedding journey lay on the bed. It was a violet satin trimmed with blue and white ribbons. The hat was of Italian straw with more blue ribbons, and there was a warm cloak to match.

Adelaide escorted her down the wide stairway to the landing where Sir William waited for them. "Two beauties," he said, with heavy gallantry. "Pamela, you look as your sister did on our wedding day, not so long ago at that!" and he kissed his wife's hand. She sent a fond glance up at him, and Pamela's throat tightened.

The marriage of Lady Adelaide Ilchester and Sir William Granby had been arranged by their parents. But from the first they had felt admiration and respect for each other. The years, their children, the closeness of their work together had deepened the respect to love. And Pamela felt jealous of that love now as she went toward her loveless marriage.

She and Douglas felt nothing but dislike for each other, she thought bitterly. How could that become anything but hate?

On the way to the church, she kept thinking frantically how she could get out of the wedding, but it was much too late now. It had probably always been too late, and she had been fighting futilely, like a small animal in a trap.

And to think she had once adored Douglas! Where had that gallant tall boy gone?

He was waiting for them at the church, remote and distinguished in a uniform of greenish blue with golden thistle decorations, and his own decorations of family crest, his medals from the wars, golden shoulder decorations of the Diplomatic. He looked like someone she had never known. And she was marrying him.

At the altar, he made his responses in a firm tone, very precise and clear to everyone. When it came her turn to speak, she felt choked up and could only mutter. He looked down at her, and she felt his arm stiffen where her hand was laid on it. She began to shake. What was she doing? Why was she meekly standing there, letting herself be married to this man who wanted another woman?

And that woman was sitting behind them in church even now. How crazy people were, she thought, her hand going blindly to her face. The veil felt stifling to her, she could not see clearly. She swayed, and felt Douglas put a quick hand to her waist to hold her.

Adelaide set back her veil, her face anxious. Douglas turned her to him, kissed her gently on the lips, his own mouth cool. Then he muttered, "Are you all right? Faint?"

"All—right," she muttered, though her vision was blurred. She longed to sit down, but the long ceremony was continuing. And then there was the reception to be gone through, long hours of standing and smiling while all of Rome seemed to have come to congratulate them and stare curiously.

She recognized some faces, others she could not. Douglas would mutter some name, or speak clearly to the person, his hand under her elbow firmly holding her up. She swayed more and more often, and finally he turned and spoke to Adelaide.

"She must sit down, she is faint."

He took her over to a sofa and brought her some champagne. She shook her head. "Water," she said faintly, and a glass of cool water was brought. She drank slowly. Her mouth was dry, her vision so blurred she thought she could not keep from falling over.

Adelaide's arm went about her, holding her firmly. "Poor dearest, it won't be long now," she whispered. "Only a few more to see, but they are important. Can you stand up?"

"I'll—try," she said raggedly. "Who—are—they—"

Douglas's voice was deep. "I'll take care of this,

don't have a care," he said crisply. He went away and she leaned her head against Adelaide's shoulder, wishing she could lie down.

Douglas brought several people back to her. She managed to sit up straight, smiled dazedly at the blur of faces, and said something, she knew not what.

Then Douglas said, "That is all, we'll go back to the villa now, and change for the journey. She should eat something—did she eat breakfast?"

"I thought so, I should have come to her earlier," said Adelaide in an agitated way.

"She has been going too madly these months," said Douglas slowly. "She shall have a rest now. I'll see to that. Come, Pamela, we'll go now."

She had thought she could not stand up without falling over. With his strong arm about her waist, she managed to walk with him to the carriage, and he set her inside tenderly. He said little on the journey to her sister's villa, and she lay back with her eyes closed.

He tucked a robe more closely about her as she shivered. He touched her hands in the little white silk gloves. "Cold as ice," he muttered.

She thought, that is what he thinks of me also —cold as ice. Well, that is what I shall be to him since he expects it.

She felt choked and put her hand to her throat. Under her palm, she felt the sharpness of the little golden thistle she had fastened inside the dress. He would never see it, she thought drearily, the little love token she had had made of his symbol.

At the house, Fanny helped her to change to the violet satin dress and had a tray brought up, as Pamela felt incapable to going to the drawing room for tea. She had eaten nothing of the elaborate wedding breakfast at the reception. Her mouth felt stiff from smiling so long.

Someone tapped on the door as she sat in a large chair, her feet up. Fanny opened the door and Douglas came in, his red hair catching the light of the candles.

He came over to Pamela. "Can you journey to-day, my dear?" he asked. "We can put it off for a few days."

She did not look at him. She thought of the elaborate arrangements, the villas ready to receive them, the dinners prepared, the horses ready at the stops. "We had best go on," she said colorlessly. "I am all right, some tea—that is all I require."

He touched her cheek with his warm fingers. She jerked her head away. He stood upright, frowning. "Well, we shall proceed, then," he said coldly. "The carriage is ready now."

Fanny bundled her into a long warm cloak, and Pamela put the hood over her hair rather than wear the straw hat. The rain was coming down in earnest now, and a more grey, sad day she had rarely seen. Adelaide kissed her goodbye, murmuring assurances that Pamela scarcely heard.

Then they set out in several grand carriages, the bride and bridegroom in one, the maids, footmen, Signora Margotti, Sir Roger Saltash, and all the luggage in the others.

Pamela leaned back and closed her eyes as soon as they had waved farewell to her sister. She thought Douglas would leave her alone and she was right. He did not speak as long as her eyes were closed.

It was not a long journey to the first stop. She felt a little refreshed by her rest, and was able to smile at her first hostess, in a villa on the edge of a small town. It was on a hill, and she much admired the view from the terrace as they awaited the elaborate dinner prepared for them. She was able to chat naturally to her hostess in Italian, and the lady was quite pleased.

When they entered the beautiful drawing room, of burgundy and gold, the hostess complimented Pamela warmly to Douglas.

"But you did not inform us that your bride spoke our tongue so fluently! What a marvel, how kind she is to trouble to learn this!"

"You must thank Signora Margotti for her patient teaching," said Pamela rather shyly, coloring under the approval in Douglas's face. Signora Margotti had joined them at table, for though she worked for a living, she was of a distinguished family. "She is instructing me in Italian history as well."

The host was politically minded, and the conversation turned to the curious situation in Germany and Austria, and the latest garbled dispatches from Napoleon's troops there. "What is Metternich up to?" the host asked.

Douglas shrugged. "If one could tell that, one would be several steps ahead of Napoleon," he said drily. "One can only hope we may discover what they are all up to, those men deciding the future of Europe."

The conversation turned serious. The hostess murmured an apology to Pamela, but the recent bride shook her head. "No, I am interested, do not distract them," she whispered back.

The dinner was long, elaborate, but interesting to Pamela, because she saw her new husband in a different light. His face was aflame with interest in his topic, and he obviously trusted his host because he spoke rather frankly with him about the future of Italy. It was late when the group finally adjourned to the drawing room, where their hostess played the piano for them.

Pamela leaned back in her wing chair, soothed and comforted by the evening. She had enjoyed the views from the villa, the long green vistas stretching about the countryside, the distant hills blue, the grey rainy skies blending into infinity. The conversation had been unexpectedly fascinating, and she had been made to feel a part of some great movement and stir. She had been treated as a woman of intelligence rather than an object to be set in a corner and taken out and dusted off now and then.

And Douglas had treated her with gentleness and courtesy, with some anxiety as to her weakness. She sat and listened to the music, her gaze on the beautiful French rug in soft cream and burgundy.

They were all silent, listening to the harpsichord. It was quite a musical family, Douglas had explained. The brother, not there at the time, played the violin and several other string instruments, and the children were learning various instruments.

It was late when they retired, but Pamela was not sorry. She had enjoyed the evening. Douglas had a room of his own next to hers, and made no gesture of coming to hers. Fanny put her to bed, and she was able to sleep rather well, wakening only a few times in the night because it was a strange room and bed.

They had a leisurely breakfast with their hosts the next morning, then set out once more, with many cordial invitations to return.

"Did you enjoy yourself, Pamela?" asked Douglas, as they set out.

"Immensely," she said warmly. "That is the

type of evening I enjoy most, with good conversation and fine music."

"I am glad that it pleased you. You do not seem so weary today. I think you have been wearying yourself too much in Rome. We shall see that you rest more in Florence."

He sounded his usual dictatorial self, and she frowned slightly. She leaned her head back against the soft cushions, and closed her eyes. If he was going to be bossy and cross with her, she would refuse to listen! But he kept silent, as she seemed to sleep.

They spent the following two evenings at villas on the way to Florence. The hosts were not always so learned and musical, but they were good friends of Douglas, and Pamela did enjoy them. Always the hospitality was of the most courteous, the food lavish, and the views from the villa grounds of splendid variety.

She much admired what she saw of the Italian scenery on the way. The mountains stretched before them and the roads were lined with varieties of green trees and cypresses that were tall and almost black. The late fall flowers glowed at various villa sites, and in the distance one could glimpse a castle on a hilltop, a formidable fortress from the Middle Ages, or a cosy country home with barns and farm animals.

But most exciting was the fourth day, when in

the late afternoon they approached the city of Florence, glowing red and cream in the late sunlight. Pamela leaned forward, peering out from the carriage, almost breathless with excitement to see the first sights of the fabulous city of which she had heard so much.

"When you are rested, we shall go down into the city, and see the Cathedral and the Bell Tower and all the famous places," Douglas promised, with a smile at her eagerness.

"Oh—that will be—marvelous," she said softly, her eyes dreamy. Florence, the city of flowers, the city of dreams. If only dreams could come true!

CHAPTER NINE

The carriages skirted Florence to climb uphill to the villa Douglas had rented. Pamela almost fell from the carriage in her eagerness to see everything on the way. Douglas caught her with strong hands and pulled her back inside as the carriage lurched again and again.

"You are like a child," he reproached her with a laugh, his face more relaxed than she had seen it recently. "I told you, tomorrow—the next day, next week—we shall see everything you wish!"

"Oh look, look at the towers, the red roofs, look at the buildings—oh, that must be the Palazzo Vecchio, it has such an odd-shaped roof and tower and the Bell Tower—oh, there is the Bell Tower!"

Patiently he pointed out other sights to her, then the road turned and twisted uphill, and Florence was lost to sight. They turned into a country lane, went about a quarter of a mile, then the carriage entered an opened gate. Servants were gathered at the doorway of the villa to greet them, young and old, even children with flowers.

She was wearing the violet dress again, with matching violet cloak and hood. As she was helped from the carriage, the hood fell back, revealing her long blond hair.

"Ah—the bella blond—bella—bella—like a blond angel," she heard the murmurs from the people. She smiled at them shyly. A small boy ran up to her, and thrust a small bunch of hyacinths into her hand, purple hyacinths. He beamed at her, then ran away.

Douglas guided her past the servants. "You will meet them all tomorrow," he said calmly, but he seemed pleased at their reception. The villa belonged to a friend and he had rented it for two months, if they cared to stay that long.

She was clutching the purple hyacinths. She lifted them to her nose, sniffing them rapturously. The delicately beautiful scent was like Florence itself, of a pure and delicate beauty. But the stems seemed stiff, and she heard them rustle. Puzzled, she glanced down, then looked more closely.

Among the stems was a twist of white paper. Her heart went cold with apprehension.

It was late evening. Who could have sent the message, who would know just when she was arriving?

"My lady?" It was the formal butler, bowing to her, gesturing the way into the villa. With Douglas following closely, she stepped into the hallway—wide, gracious, and gleaming with lightly polished woods.

At any other time, her heart would have leaped with pleasure to see the lovely home. The hall was hung with portraits, the stairs were circular, winding up to the landing on the next floor. She was conducted first into a formal drawing room where tea was laid. The carpets were rare and thick, of glowing ruby and emerald colors. The furniture was sturdy, elegantly carved, with satin and plush seats.

She clung to the purple hyacinths, and set the bunch into her lap when a servant would have taken them from her. "No, I wish to smell them, they are marvelous," she said with a smile.

She drank a little tea and ate some cakes. Douglas told her that dinner would be served in an hour, in case she wished to retire early.

"Yes, I am—quite weary," she said, drooping a little. She was not nearly as tired as on her wedding day. She had rested even during their journey, it had been made so easy and so pleasant.

Presently she was conducted up to her own rooms. She had a large pleasant sitting room looking onto a balcony, which in turn gave glorious views of the formal box gardens below. Her bedroom of blue and rose was the size of a small gymnasium, she thought with some humor. It was hung with elegant tapestries in faded silks, with mythological scenes she would puzzle out later. Her bath also was huge, with white tiles and white porcelain decorated with roses.

Fanny was there to make her comfortable in a fresh dress for evening. While the maid was unpacking, Pamela retired to the bathroom, the hyacinths still clutched in her hand. She opened the stems and extracted the white paper.

She untwisted the page, then frowned over the words. Finally she deciphered the Italian scrawl. "My lady, I beg you, I am wounded and feverish. I was shot. Bring medicine, salve, bandages, some money—I am desperate. Paolo, the boy, will wait in the gardens and conduct you. Aid me or I die. C."

"My God, my dear God," she whispered. She stared at the scribble. Carlo must indeed be desperate or he would never have sent such a plea. She bit her lips. Medicine, salve, bandages. Had Fanny unpacked enough? She opened a handbag on a porcelain stand, and sighed with relief. Yes, the medicines she always carried, and bandages for scratches, they would have to do. Shot? Was the bullet still in him? She must take sharp scissors. What else?

"My lady?" called Fanny anxiously. "My lord asks if you are ready for dinner."

"Just five more minutes!" she called back. Feverishly, she set the things she would require into a large scarf and put it into the handbag. She went back into the bedroom to find her lord waiting for her, looming large even in the huge room. She stiffened in alarm. Would he feel free to invade her bedroom when he chose?

"Would you set these in a small vase near the bed, Fanny, please?" She handed the flowers to Fanny and turned with a smile to Douglas. "I adore those hyacinths, they are like Florence. I am sure I shall enjoy it here."

His face relaxed again. He always watched her face so closely that it made her uneasy. He seemed to study her constantly.

"I hope you shall enjoy it immensely," he said gravely. "Florence is one of my favorite cities. Shall we go down to dinner?"

She took his arm, her hand lightly on his sleeve. Even with the cloth between them, she could feel his hardness and strength. Would it ever be turned against her? Her heart seemed to hurt her with its rapid beating.

They went down the winding staircase to the dining room where they found Sir Roger Saltash and Signora Margotti waiting for them. Pamela was relieved; the last thing she wanted to do was dine alone with her formidable new husband.

Feverishly, she chatted of the journey, the villa, the wonders of Florence. Signora Margotti aided her with placid commentary on the art objects, and the sights which might be of most interest. Roger contributed an amiable vague chorus of pleasure at being in one of Europe's most artistic cities. Douglas said little, apparently absorbed in the excellent veal, fresh vegetables, and hot coffee.

But every now and then she caught his keen eyes gazing at her face, and wondered nervously what he was thinking.

They retired to the drawing room for brandy and more coffee. She poured for them, then sat back on the sofa. She felt keyed up, tense, apprehensive. She closed her eyes for a long moment, and opened them to find Douglas studying her face again.

"You are very weary, I think, Pamela," he said softly, as Signora Margotti chatted to Roger about the work of Michaelangelo. "I am sorry about that. I had hoped the journey would be easy enough to rest you."

"It was easy, very enjoyable," she said brightly.

"But I believe you are right, I overdid it in Rome. I am still quite weary."

"I shall insist on supervising your activities from now on," he said without a smile, his look serious and intent. "Adelaide allowed you to run about too much, you were much spoiled by her, I believe."

She stiffened, resenting that. "She has always cared for me," she said coldly. "Since my parents died, she has been both sister and mother."

"I believe that. Nonetheless, she allowed you to run about and weary yourself. I do not think she understood that your strength has its limits. And Italy is more conventional than England."

She bit her lip, staring down at her coffee cup. Her gentler feelings toward him were undergoing a violent change once more. He was being dictatorial. But he would find her not so easy to handle!

Signora Margotti soon excused herself tactfully. Roger then followed her lead, and excused himself to go to his rooms. Pamela looked up at Douglas when they were finally alone. He had assumed his favorite stance, lounging at the mantel and gazing down into the fire, his coffee cup near him.

"I wonder if you would excuse me also, Douglas?" she forced herself to say quietly, almost meekly. "I am extremely weary, and would like to retire—by myself."

He turned, and she looked him directly in the

eyes. He studied her for a long moment. "Of course, Pamela, I understand," he said. "Would you like to go up to your rooms now?"

She rose at once, shaking out her skirts gracefully. "I will say goodnight, then," she said.

He accompanied her to the door, and she was burningly conscious of his gaze on her as she walked slowly up the stairs alone. When she had turned the final curve of the staircase, and he could no longer see her, she went limp, and had to hang on to the bannister for a moment before going up the last few steps.

She went to the room. Fanny had laid out her nightdress and robe and disappeared, leaving only a few candles burning. Pamela's mouth twisted. She did not expect a romantic wedding night tonight!

She quickly changed to a dark dress of serviceable serge she sometimes used to garden. Over it she put her black cloak with black hood. She picked up the large scarf of bandages and medicines, and was ready. She had observed the back stairs, and thought she could find her way readily to the gardens.

Quietly she opened her door, listened, then drew it shut after her. She stole to the back stairway and crept down it. She could hear the rapid Italian of servants in the kitchens—chatting, laughing, scolding. She waited until the back hall was clear, then scurried across it to a side door she found.

She opened it, and was in the gardens. The first garden was the vegetable garden, and she made her way across very cautiously. Then she was in the first of several flower gardens, rimmed about with trimmed box hedges.

She walked on slowly, keeping the hood closely about her head and face. She started violently when a small hand touched her hand with the thick scarf in it.

"Signora—my lady—it is I, Paolo," whispered a voice. She looked down to make out in the dimness the eager face of the small boy who had given her the hyacinths.

"Where is Carlo?" she whispered.

"I take you there!" He tugged at her hand imperiously. He was such a small messenger! But he seemed to know just what he was doing. He took her rapidly through more gardens, beyond to a forest, and out a wire fence to a small shed some distance from the house.

All was darkness. She was momentarily afraid, then she heard a familiar voice. "My lady? Is it you?"

"Carlo," she breathed. The voice had been so weak. She groped in the darkness, then the boy lit a candle and placed it near the form of the man lying on some sacks in the shed.

She knelt down and touched his forehead. It was burning hot. "How long have you been here?"

"Six days," he breathed weakly. "My God, I cannot believe—you are a miracle. I waited. I knew your plans. It was the only hope. Someone betrayed me—"

Deftly, she opened his bloody shirt. Paolo held the candle higher and closer for her to see and she bit her lips to hold back angry words. The wound was stiff with blood, hot and feverish to the touch.

"The bullet—it is inside?" she whispered.

"Si, Signora. Inside."

She probed gently with her small fingers. He sighed in a moan of pain, which he tried to stifle. "I think it is not too deep. I must remove it, Carlo."

"Si, Signora," he agreed simply. "You brought something?"

She took out the scissors and knife, and the small bottle of brandy. She gave him some brandy, then poured some on the instruments, as an army doctor had once instructed her. She did not know what it did, but it seemed to help the wound, he had told her.

The operation was long and painful. Carlo was in a weakened condition and he finally fainted. His timid doctor, trembling, shaking with fear of doing the wrong thing, finally managed to probe for the bullet with the knife, and use both scissors and knife to lift it out. She heard Paolo grunting beside her in sympathy with her every move.

When the bullet came out, he sighed, "Oh, *brava, brava!* You are such a one I never saw!"

She laughed shakily, and sat back on her heels, trying to recover. She looked down tenderly at the smooth pallid face of the unconscious man, and wiped her hands on the scarf. She took the bottle of water Paolo offered, and bathed his lips and face and head. Carlo was so hot, so very hot.

"When did he last eat?" she whispered to the boy.

His shoulders lifted in a small imitation of the typical Italian gesture, his hands out, palms up. "Who knows? I leave bread and meat and water for him. He can eat little for the fever. He needs hot soup, hot coffee, hot tea."

"Do you think you could steal back to the kitchen, after everyone is asleep, and heat some soup on the stove?"

He thought about it, then nodded. "Si, Signora. I do it."

They sat beside the unconscious man for a time, Pamela bathing his forehead and looking at the wound anxiously, worried about him. He needed much more attention, but who could she trust?

The water supply was low. Paolo whispered, "I get more from the pump," and returned with a pan full. She bathed Carlo's forehead and the wound and thought he seemed easier.

Presently Paolo disappeared, to return a long time later carefully carrying a small pan of hot soup. She did not ask him how he managed. They woke up Carlo, fed him some mouthfuls, and Paolo hungrily ate the rest with some bread.

Then they waited again.

"Is there anyone who can help him? Can you get hot soup and bread from anyone?" she finally whispered.

"My mother will let me have some, but our money is low," he murmured, his head down.

She took out money from the pocket of her cloak. "There—take it all—"

He drew back. "Oh no, Signora, she would be suspicious if I have so much. Give me this much—" And he deftly took a small amount from the handful. Carlo smiled weakly.

"That one, he is so clever already," he said feebly. "I am much the better now, Signora. You must return to the villa before you are missed."

"I will wait until almost dawn, and care for you," she said quietly. She bathed his face again, and smiled down at him. His face was rough with beard, his eyes were drawn, and his body smelled of the sweat of his fever. But she admired his courage, his daring. "You have done so much, will you deny me the privilege of doing a little?"

He took her hand weakly, and raised it to his feverish lips. "You are—a lady—" he said, and lay back as though the effort had exhausted him.

She waited until the light in the east was growing before she stole back to the house. The servants would soon be about, and she must be back in her rooms by that time. She had crammed the scarf and knife and scissors in her pocket. If they found her, she would say she was taking an early morning walk.

But no one saw her as she went up the back stairs to her rooms. She opened the door softly to her sitting room, and went inside. The rooms were still, just lighting with the morning dawn. She crept to the huge bedroom, went inside.

Then she saw that the door to Douglas's rooms was opened from her bedroom! And as she stared, Douglas came to the door. He was wearing his robe of a greenish blue with a golden thistle embroidered on the chest.

His red hair was ruffled, his eyes rimmed with red from lack of sleep. His eyes were very green and hard as he stared at her, taking in the muddy slippers, the dusty cloak, her general disarray.

"Where have you been, Pamela?" he asked coldly, ominously. He stepped further into her room. She backed up nervously, until stopped by the door to her sitting room.

"I—I went out for—for an early morning walk—" she said brazenly, meeting his glance bravely.

"All night?" he asked. He was angry with a deadly anger she had never seen before. "I came to your room soon after you had retired. You were gone then. You have not been back. Where were you?"

She stared at him, her throat dry. She could not speak.

"You will not say? Why, Pamela? Where did you go? Whom did you meet? Answer!" He did not raise his voice. He was controlled, deadly controlled and cold.

"I—cannot—tell—you," she whispered.

He stared at her, then turned and went back to his room. He closed the door gently. She found it more ominous than if he had slammed it. She began to shiver, and could not stop.

CHAPTER TEN

Pamela went to bed as the sun was rising. She was cold for a long time, shivering in the huge strange bed, until finally her exhaustion overcame her and she slept.

She did not awake until late afternoon. When she opened her eyes, she could not remember for a time where she was. She gazed about the room with sleepy curiosity, blinking at the huge French windows, the drawn curtains.

From somewhere she heard bells chiming, as though from a great distance, like bells chimed and struck and hummed from under the sea. She wondered what it could be, then she remembered.

She was in Florence! When they had arrived

the previous afternoon, the bells had been chiming. They could be heard from the city below them in the valley of the Arno, all the church and cathedral bells ringing in the early evening, like a joyful humming from the beautiful rooftops and cypress trees below them.

Presently Fanny opened the door cautiously, and came in with a smile when she saw her mistress was awake.

"Laws, my lady, how you did sleep! Do you know you missed everything from breakfast to tea? You'll get a good rest here, I'll warrant!" And she bustled about cheerfully as Pamela drank a cup of hot tea sitting up in bed.

She laid out an evening dress of palest blue muslin trimmed in white lace. Pamela shook her head.

"No, Fanny, get out something warmer. It will be cold here, I think. What about the red velvet dress with gold?"

Fanny hesitated. "I think your husband admires you most in blue, my lady," she finally said, delicately.

"Another time, Fanny," said Pamela curtly. She had a lovely blue velvet, but she did not mean to wear it, not for Douglas! She put on the red velvet defiantly, wore her hair severely upswept, and prepared to go downstairs.

The others were gathered in the drawing room.

Signora Margotti and Roger Saltash were discussing something about art as she came in. They stopped talking and turned to greet her with a smile. Douglas turned from his pose in front of the mantel. He was unsmiling, severe, almost frowning. He came forward after a pause to greet her. He took her hand, looking down at her keenly.

"You are feeling quite better, Pamela?" he asked rather curtly, his voice unusually deep.

"I had a good sleep, yes," she said evasively. She did not mean to assure him she felt quite well. She slipped her slim hand from his as he did not let it go quite soon enough to please her. She turned to Roger, smiled at him, and said, "How are you? Are you feeling dull already in the country?"

"How can you say so, my lady?" he said formally but with an answering smile. "Signora Margotti and I are busily arguing over which sights you shall see first! You must permit us to plan a busy schedule for you!"

"I want her to rest first," said Douglas, as though he could not be argued with.

"Of course, naturally," said Signora Margotti, in her diplomatic fashion. "Then, later, we must visit the art galleries, the shops, the cafés. Perhaps we might attend the cathedral services on Sunday."

"That sounds enchanting," said Pamela, going to sit on the sofa beside the Signora. She arranged her full red velvet skirts carefully. She must think how to see Carlo tonight. She did not dare go in the daylight when she might be seen and followed. His enemies were probably about.

Douglas, after the first expression of concern, seemed to turn cold and indifferent. At dinner he spoke little, apparently absorbed in his own thoughts. He and Roger said a few words about some work that was being sent up to them from Rome, some papers to be redrawn.

Pamela absorbed herself in conversation with Signora Margotti and encouraged the tactful woman to treat her to long lectures on the various art objects they would encounter on the sight-seeing. She tried to listen carefully to the explanations of the art of Michaelangelo and Leonardo da Vinci and some of the other Tuscan artists, but she found herself glancing uneasily at her husband at the other end of the table.

He was so very stern and hard-looking, she thought. His face seemed carved in light tan wood, his red hair flaming above the icy green eyes. He was very angry with her. Well, let him be. It would keep him from her, and perhaps he would soon return to Rome and his Beata!

The thought seemed to stab her, and she caught her breath. She touched the front of her velvet gown lightly. Why, why did she still wear the golden thistle brooch? She should put it away in her jewelry box wrapped in a cloth, and forget it. Such sentiment was finished.

The dinner was finally over, and they returned to the drawing room. Pamela's efforts at conversation were labored. She kept thinking more and more uneasily about Carlo. Had she managed to reduce the fever? Would Paolo be able to bring hot soup to him? Would he be discovered? What could she do to rescue him? She must take blankets to him tonight, the weather was much colder, and those thin grain sacks would not protect him.

"There is a book that describes the art much more effectively than I can," Signora Margotti finally offered gently. "Would you like me to read from it and translate for you?"

She brought the book to Pamela, a small, elaborately bound volume in purple leather. Pamela glanced at it, and returned it to the Signora.

"Would you read to us in Italian, Signora? That would be good practice for me. However, I do not know if my lord wishes—" She glanced up at Douglas from under her lashes as she spoke of him formally.

He came over from the mantel, and sat down in a huge satin armchair near them. "Please, do read to us, Signora. That would be pleasant."

So the evening passed without incident. The

Signora patiently read to them in Italian, pausing to explain an obscure or technical word or phrase, then continuing, until Roger was yawning behind his hand.

They all retired early. Pamela allowed herself to be partially undressed by Fanny, then dismissed the maid, saying she wished to read for a time. She picked up the volume she had brought from the library, ignoring the maid's surprise, and began to read.

When the villa was quiet and she heard no sounds from her husband in the next bedroom, she got up quietly and dressed in the dark gown. She put on cloak and hood, and carrying several dark blankets and bandages, salve, and brandy, she set out. She managed to get to Carlo without incident, Paolo intercepting her in the gardens, beaming all over his small face.

"Ah, Signora, you come again. *Brava!* I brought him hot soup today. He is better."

"Good, good," she whispered back, relieved. They went to Carlo's shed, and she entered. Paolo lit a small candle, and came in also.

Carlo's eyes were bright with fever, but he smiled at seeing her. She touched his forehead gently. He did not seem quite so hot today. She spread out the blankets, arranged them, put him inside. He shuddered in relief at the warmth.

"Ah, how good, how good that is," he muttered

in Italian. "You are so very very kind, my lady."

She dressed the wound, then spoke to Carlo in whispers about the danger.

"Does anyone else know you are here? Is Paolo ever followed?"

"He is followed. But he is clever, he gets away. But they might find me. However, there is a chance. When I am better, I can move to another place I know."

She worried about it, her eyebrows drawn together in a frown. "I will come every night," she whispered. "It is our garden here, the villa is rented from friends. If I am discovered, I can say I am taking a night walk. My husband will be infuriated, but he will back up my story."

"Your husband? The Earl of Fitzroy? He is a good man, I think," said Carlo weakly. "However, he is in the Diplomatic, you should not confide in him. He does not know—" His anxious look completed the question.

She shook her head, flushing as she remembered Douglas's anger at dawn. "No, and I will not tell him," she said flatly.

Carlo breathed a sigh of relief, and turned slightly on his hard earthen bed. "Ah, the blankets, so good," he murmured again, contentedly.

Her heart hurt her, when she thought of her huge comfortable bed, the large luxurious warm room, the huge bath. Carlo was grateful for food, a few blankets, a little salve for his wound.

She returned to her room, without being seen she thought, then went out again the next night, and the next. Her husband seemed quite cold and indifferent to her. He did not attempt to come to her bedroom, day or night. She saw him only in the formal rooms of the villa as he did not even come to her sitting room.

She felt quite rested within a few days, and Douglas approved of a small expedition to Florence. He accompanied her, however, and went with her and Signora Margotti to the art galleries, the cafés, the excellent restaurants. He proved almost as good a guide as the Signora, and between them, Pamela began to learn a great deal about Florence. It was delightful.

She loved the small brown winding streets, the tall grey stone buildings which loomed from the Middle Ages and Renaissance like city-forts. She looked long at the strong faces of the portraits and sculpture busts of the Medici, the condottieri, warriors of the past.

She went again and again, every two or three days. Sometimes Douglas went with them or sometimes Roger was commissioned to go with them, as though under orders, Pamela thought resentfully.

Roger was quite pleasant company, however, and when she wished to sit and sketch for hours, he would be silent or only murmur little words to Signora Margotti. Both seemed quite pleased to sit in outdoor cafés with her, idly dreaming or talking, or looking at the passers-by as she worked at her drawing.

The days went rapidly by. The only flaw—a huge one, she had to admit to herself—was the coldness between herself and Douglas. He worked in his study much of the day. He spent the evenings with them in one of the drawing rooms, and as the days and evenings grew colder, he often stood at the fireplace warming his hands and gazing at them absently, scarcely seeing them.

She took more blankets to Carlo. The nights were freezing cold, especially up here on the hill. His strength increased, but he was still unable to stand without help.

Then Paolo came to her in the garden one afternoon as she strolled in her cloak.

"Signora, Signora," he whispered. One of the gardeners started toward them, as though to keep her from being pestered. She waved him back imperiously, took Paolo's hand, and drew him with her to where a fountain plashed in the chill air.

The child looked so pale and anxious, she knew at once what had happened.

"What is it? Tell me quickly," she whispered, clenching his hand tightly in hers.

"They discovered his place, last night. I helped

him move away in the bushes, but he could take only one blanket. They are looking about today for him."

She was silent, her mouth tight. "We must find another place," she said at last.

"There is another, a cave, further in the hills. But he cannot walk. He is so weak. I cannot carry him," murmured the small boy, his head down, as though he had failed.

She could not carry Carlo either, she thought. He was slim, but too tall. She would never manage. Whom could she ask for help?

"Roger," she thought. Yes, Roger. He would be guided by her. He was not a strong man in moral courage, but he would do what she asked and be silent. She knew enough about him now to realize that. He was weak compared to Douglas, but perhaps weak men were nicer, sweeter companions.

"Meet me here at midnight," she said finally. "I will bring a man with me who will help us move Carlo." She nodded to the boy, sent him away decisively, then went back to the house.

She managed to find Roger alone for a few moments in the drawing room later in the evening.

"I need your help," she said, without giving him a chance to refuse. "Meet me here at the French doors just before midnight."

He went pale. "Meet—*you?*" he asked weakly. "But Pamela—my lady—if he found out—"

"This is not a romantic assignation," she said curtly, and left him.

He kept looking at her in puzzled fashion all that evening, and in her impatience she could have slapped him. She wished he were strong like Douglas—but no, Douglas was cold and hard. She did not like any man to be like that! Better weakness than such iciness.

She thought the evening would never end. She cut it short by retiring early, then was sorry, because the hours seemed endless as she read in her bedroom. She had sent Fanny away. She kept hearing Douglas in his bedroom, and thought twice he was coming into her room. She could hear him pacing.

Finally all was quiet. At midnight, she slipped out of her room, down the back stairs, out into the hallway. She went to the drawing room, shrouded and mysterious in the night quiet. She went through the room, to the French windows, out onto the cold terrace, and waited.

She wore a warm dress, and her cloak under it. She carried two blankets, thinking it might be easier to carry Carlo in them.

Finally a figure materialized beside her. "What is it?" whispered Roger nervously. His hand caught hers, it was cold. "What are you doing, Pamela?"

"You will see," she said curtly. "Come along!"

She pulled him with her, down into the gardens, and through the box hedges to the fountain.

"But what—" he was beginning, when Paolo appeared beside him and made him jump. The small boy looked up at the man gravely, as though judging him critically. Roger stared down at the boy in turn. "Who is he?"

"Shush! Come along. Lead us, Paolo. This is Sir Roger Saltash. He will go with us, and not speak of the matter!"

"Si, my lady," said Paolo, but he sounded doubtful. He turned and led them along paths and country lanes for quite a long distance. Finally he unexpectedly opened some bushes and showed them where Carlo lay.

Roger leaned over Carlo, staring aghast at him in the dim light of the moon and star-sprinkled sky. "But who—why, it is Carlo da Ponte. Man, what happened to you?"

"He was shot and is still weak and feverish," said Pamela briefly. "We are going to move him to safety. Paolo, carry this blanket, we will wrap Carlo in the others."

"I can walk—with help," said Carlo weakly. "If you would but help me up—"

Pamela leaned over and gave him the strong support of her young body, lifting him up, holding with her arm about his waist until the faintness went away.

"Take the other side, Roger, help him," she directed. Paolo picked up the other blankets, and managed them all, with small pots and pans, bandages, salve. Then the boy led the way, along narrow paths, under the trees, out briefly into the open, and on and on.

Finally Carlo stopped. "Are you weak?" asked Pamela very gently.

"No, I shall stop here. I thank you, my lady. Leave me here with Paolo. It is not safe for you, my lady, to know where I will be. I thank you, and I shall contact you later if necessary. May God thank and bless you for your kindness." He managed to lift her hand to his lips.

"But I want to help you—" she began, then paused. It was not safe for Carlo for too many to know of his true hiding place. And Paolo had enough money to buy food and medicine for him. "Yes," she said. "God bless you, Carlo. Contact me again if you need me. I shall always help you."

He sighed and smiled at her. "What have I done to deserve such magnificent help?"

"You have been courageous," she said simply. "Farewell. God keep you, and your cause." She bent, and lightly kissed his unshaven cheek.

Roger had been silent. Now he wrung Carlo's hand and followed Pamela into the darkness. She found her way back by instinct and followed the dim trail through the forest. They arrived at the villa road, and went slowly up to the terrace.

"No talking tonight," she said wearily, as they arrived at the French windows. "Of course, we cannot tell anyone—"

"Of course. You may trust me," he assured her. "We will speak in the morning of this—"

"Pamela? Roger? What are you doing here? It is almost three in the morning!"

Douglas stood in the open French window!

CHAPTER ELEVEN

He was no longer cool. He was fiery hot, blazingly angry. Pamela stood in appalled silence as his wrath blasted over both their heads.

"What the hell do you think you are doing with my wife?" he raged at Roger. "Do you imagine I would stand still while you kept a shoddy little assignation with her? You are a dolt! And you, Pamela. I thought you were young and giddy, but I never imagined you to be a cheat and a doxy! You might at least have chosen someone with strength of character, and enough intelligence not to carry on an affair under my nose. No! Be silent!" he roared, as Roger attempted to speak.

Pamela stood rigidly as he yelled at both of them.

"So you are too weary to stay up at night!" he told Pamela, ferociously. "No wonder! Your wanderings at night must keep you quite busy and use up all your strength! I wonder at you! How many men do you require to amuse you? Do you reward them suitably? I never imagined a girl such as you were as a child would grow up to be such a chit!"

Now she finally spoke. "That is enough!" she said with cold fury. "You have no right to call me such names! You do not know the circumstances, and I shall not reveal them to you. But do not speak to me in this manner!"

"I shall speak to you as I think suitable! You are in my care, God help me! Why I ever married you—"

"I tried to stop the wedding," she said with some relish and more than a little spite. "You would not listen to me!"

"Why didn't you reveal you had taken a lover —or two, or three?" he flared back at her. "It might have been more persuasive an argument! No, you must speak vaguely of not being suitable. I never thought you a flirt, a cheat, a liar!"

She wanted to strike him. She was so furiously angry that she would have hit out blindly. Roger was moving nervously behind her.

"I say—we haven't, that is—it wasn't like that," he managed to stammer. "We were helping—that is—"

"Be quiet, Roger!" Pamela turned on him in anger and dismay. "This is not your secret. Be quiet!"

Roger still stammered on. "It isn't—I mean—not romance, I assure you, Kinnair! I would never —I mean, she is your wife, and all that—"

"Thank you so very much for remembering that, even though it be late!" Douglas's voice was still taut with rage.

"But we had to help Carlo—"

The words were out. Pamela turned on Roger. "You—how can you? This was in confidence—"

"Carlo? You mean, Carlo da Ponte? What has he to do with this?" asked Douglas keenly, on the scent.

Pamela shivered. "You—it is not your affair. You are best—best out of this—" she stammered. She should have known better than to entrust such a mission to weakling Roger.

"Come inside," Douglas said quietly, taking her arm and drawing her into the drawing room. "Who was it, Roger? Whom did you meet?"

"Well, it was Carlo da Ponte. He was wounded, you see, quite feverish, and everyone on the alert for him, had to hide out, you see—"

Pamela said desperately, "Roger, if you say

one more word, I shall strike you! You are no gentleman!"

Douglas looked at them both in the dim light of the drawing room. Then he said, "Roger, leave us. Pamela, we shall go upstairs to your rooms and speak where no one can hear us. I will know the whole truth of this matter!"

Roger escaped with haste. Douglas took Pamela by the arm under her cloak, and his grip was like steel. "We will go upstairs."

She was forced to accompany him. She despised her weakness, hated that she was trembling. She told herself that it was weariness, that she had not had enough sleep, that the trip carrying Carlo had been almost beyond her strength. But she knew it was more than that, it was some violent emotion she felt when Douglas touched her, when he turned the full strength of his attention upon her. He could look at her across a room, and she would feel a chill or a fever, a strange weakness inside.

He took her up to her rooms, and closed the door after them. The villa was silent, as though only the two of them were awake. The candles had burned down, but there was enough yet in their length for a few more hours.

She took off her cloak and hood slowly, with shaking hands. He made no move to help her, watching in ominous silence as she set the cloak on a chair. She seated herself in a chair and he sat down opposite.

"I am waiting, Pamela," he said frigidly.

She looked at him, her lips closed, taut.

"You will explain where you went. How often have you seen Carlo da Ponte? What relationship is there between you?"

She would not answer. He glared at her, his eyes flashing in the candlelight.

"That first night here at the villa," he said after a pause, "were you out all night with Carlo—or with Roger?"

She lowered her gaze to her slim hands, gripped in her lap. If she did not tell him anything, he would have no weapons against her.

"Pamela," he said, almost gently. "If you do not answer my questions, I will make you very sorry!"

"Do you mean to beat me, sir?" she asked pertly, her violet eyes flashing with as much rage as his green.

"Perhaps! Do not drive me too far! Answer my questions! Have you seen Carlo many times since we came? Did you meet him often in Rome?"

She looked down again at her hands. They twisted and turned, and she found herself fingering the wedding ring and the heavy gold and emerald engagement ring on her slim finger.

"Pamela. Do you remember when you tried to ride the black stallion? When he would not obey you? Do you remember what happened?"

She nodded reluctantly, her lips compressed.

There had been a black stallion in her father's stable. She had been forbidden to ride him, but she wanted to, and with the reluctant help of a groom, she had taken him out.

Douglas had found them, riding like crazy on the fields, through a small grove. He had cut them off, turned the wild animal, snatched Pamela from its back like a child, and scolded her thorougly.

"This time you have taken on more than you can handle with your small hands," he said quietly. "If you are aiding a spy, that is sufficient to expel us from Italy."

"And that is all you care about," she flashed. "You care nothing for the Italian cause! The cause of a free Italy, independent of Austria, yes, and of Britain!"

There was a heavy silence. She regretted her impulsive words as soon as they were spoken.

"As a member of the Diplomatic on a delicate mission, I cannot afford to care for the fate of a single Italian spy," he said slowly, as though with some regret. "Carlo da Ponte is a dangerous man. He is a very clever spy, he learned much in Sir William's careless handling of his papers. If it is learned that you are aiding him, Pamela, we shall have to leave Italy. And my mission is potentially worth more than—" He paused.

"More than our marriage? But anything is worth more than that! Our marriage is a mockery! I tried to stop it. You are obsessed with that— that Beata Lanza! You should have married her! At the least, you should not have inflicted me with—"

"Be careful! Have a care of your tongue, woman!" he warned, his tone dangerous. "You know why I married you. I promised your father years ago that I would take care of you, no matter what the cost! Your parents would weep now if they could see what you are becoming!"

She flung up her head furiously. "How dare you! They would be proud of me! They taught me to think for myself, not accept the dictatorial statements of—of any man! And I will not be so insulted! Leave me! Go to your own rooms! Tomorrow, I shall leave you, and return to my sister's house!"

She jumped up, so angry she did not count the cost. He was near her in an instant, and his hand gripped her slim wrist so hard that his fingers overlapped around it.

"You drive a man hard!" he said between his teeth. "You tempt him with your beauty, you madden him with your coldness, then you insult—" He tried to pull her closer to him.

"Let me go!" She was more angry than frightened, and she fought him fiercely. "I hate you! I despise you! You speak of me—but what of you? Or is a man allowed to carry on affairs, have mistresses, and the world looks the other way? What of you? Why should I not have pleasure where I choose? I am free!"

"You are not free! You belong to me!" He pulled her closer to him, and suddenly she was aware that he was aroused and dangerous. He was not fighting her to hurt her, he wanted her!

His arms were about her, he had pulled her to his warm body. They fought silently, and angrily. She wrenched herself free, but her arm was pulled, her right arm, so that it stung. She flung about, fought free again, only to be grabbed back into his arms. He fought her over to the couch and pushed her down, she kicked at him violently, striking at him with her free hand.

"No, no, no!" she panted, as he tried to force a kiss on her mouth. She looked at that hard stern mouth, and vowed she would die before she let it touch her willingly. "I hate you! I hate you!"

"Tell me something new!" he mocked her, and again his mouth was near hers. She turned her head to one side, he caught at her chin, held her still for a moment, and succeeded in pressing a hotly angry kiss on her mouth. It stung as though he had struck her.

"You—you are no gentleman! You—bully! Beast!" She panted the words, struck at him, kicked at him with her sharp shoes. He pushed her again into the cushions of the velvet couch, bent over her so that his warm body was pressing hers, and tried to force another kiss on her.

"Hold still," he muttered.

She wriggled and twisted. She was weary but she would not give in. She fought him fiercely, with all her frail strength. She learned the toughness of his body, the strength in his hard arms and legs as he fought her for the embrace.

"Go—to—Beata!" she cried out.

It infuriated him. He held her still, and for a long moment, his lips held her silent. His mouth opened against hers, and she felt a dangerous weakness thrilling through her body, as his arms held her to him, his open mouth claimed hers brutally.

She fought both her own weakness and his strength. She would not be raped! Her arms wrestled with his, she pushed at his chest, she struck at his face, her fingers like talons.

"Little devil!" he muttered, and had to concentrate on merely holding her as she tried to slip from his grip. They fought across the couch, slid to the floor, landing with a thud which hurt her hip. Still she struck at him, until with one hand on each wrist he held her motionless. His body was weighing hers down, he was on her, his leg across her legs. The dress had ridden up high, to her thighs, and she burned with shame and fury.

"No—no—no," she panted. She twisted, until she infuriated him again. He held her arm hard as she tried to twist. She cried out. The arm had turned, wrenching her left arm until it was across her body, about to snap.

"Oh—you hurt me—you hurt—"

He let go her arm, and put his hand to her throat. She thought he would kill her, he was so angry. Instead, his fingers caught hold of the fabric of her dress at the collar, and he wrenched it downward!

The dress held until her neck hurt, then it gave way. The fabric ripped down, down, to her waist, down to the hem, and he pulled it back roughly. Her neck stung and burned, her arm was so painful that it brought tears to her eyes.

"You must give in to me," he muttered. "You must—" And his lips sought hers greedily.

She was so hurt and so bruised that she began to cry. Tears streamed down her cheeks, and she sobbed aloud. She could not fight him any longer, she was so bruised and aching. "No, no, no," she said weakly, as his mouth pressed to hers, then released it. "No, no, no, you hurt me—you hurt me—"

She heard him mutter something inaudible, and his arms were still. He sat up, from his posture on the floor crouched over her. He said, more clearly, "My God, what am I doing?"

She lay and wept, crouched in a little ball of pain. Her arm hurt so, and she ached all over. She felt his hands on her waist, and she thought he was attacking again.

"Oh God, let me go, let me go, haven't you hurt me enough?" she sobbed.

She felt him stiffen. His hands went over her. Then he got up and bent to her. "Let me help you up, Pamela," he said, very quietly. "Pamela?"

"No—let me alone—let me alone—" She turned her wet face from him, still in the crouched ball of pain. She hugged her arm to her.

She heard him give a deep heavy sigh. He got up, and walked away. She stifled her sobbing against her good arm, crouched, leaning against the sofa. She was so tired, so tired—

He came back, carrying something thick and soft, one of her robes. He bent over her, took the torn dress from her. "Put this on, Pamela," he said gently.

Wearily, she let herself be raised, and he put the robe about her and set her down on the couch. He was gazing down at her as he began to fasten the soft belt of the robe. He paused. He was staring at her, staring—

He put his hand to her bosom. She winced, trying to lean back away from him. His brown fingers touched the golden thistle brooch fastened to her undergarment.

"What is this?" he asked.

She hung her head sullenly. She vowed she would never wear that again! She hated him with such passion and fierce violence as she had never felt in her life. He was a bully, a beast, domineering, a tyrant—

"What is this, Pamela? It looks like a golden thistle, my symbol. Where did you get it?"

She would not answer. He finally sat down beside her, looked at her, then silently took out his large white handkerchief and began to mop her face from the tears.

"Where did I hurt you?" he asked quietly. "Your arm? Your left arm?"

She nodded. He took the arm in his hands and examined the shoulder and upper arm, moving the robe back to look at it.

"Bruised. And did I wrench it?"

She nodded. She would not look at his face. The tenderness and anxiety in his tone had no power to touch her, she thought.

"I am sorry, Pamela. I was infuriated, but I had no reason to forget that I am a gentleman, and you are a lady. Forgive me?"

She did not answer. She would never forgive him!

"I was too rough, far too rough. Will you not look at me, my dear?" He took her chin in his fingers and tried to turn her head toward him. Her neck hurt and she winced. When he turned her head anyway, she closed her eyes tightly, rejecting him with her every gesture.

"Well, we will talk tomorrow. It is very late, and you are weary. But you must tell me all about what you have been doing, for I shall not tolerate this business with Carlo da Ponte. And involving Roger in your schemes! This is dangerous work, Pamela! I shall have to scold you—but let that wait until tomorrow. Go to bed now."

She shrank back from him as he would have lifted her. "Only when you leave me," she said frigidly.

"Do you have some salve for your arm? Shall I get some?"

"I have all that is necessary! Leave me!"

He still hesitated, gazing down at her, as he sat beside her. "Pamela, where did you get the brooch?"

She bit her lips.

"Have you had it long?" He touched it again with his fingers. She hated having him so close, almost touching her breast.

"I will tell you if you promise to leave my room!"

"I promise—for tonight," he said, his mouth hard.

"I had it made years ago—when we were first engaged! When I thought you other than you are!" she said furiously.

"And you have worn it since? There?" He indicated the place.

She glared at him. He finally rose, and said, "Goodnight, Pamela. I will see you in the morning. But sleep long, you need more rest. We shall speak of this when we are more calm."

CHAPTER TWELVE

Pamela slept poorly that night. The salve had not relieved the severe pain in her left arm, nor the ache in her neck. She thought she had never in her life hated anyone so much.

Wars and battles must have changed Douglas and women like Beata. Maybe she enjoyed his bullying ways, his beastliness, his roughness. Well, his wife would not endure such behavior! He must go to his mistress for that!

She was awake when Fanny came softly into her room the next morning. She sat up wearily for her tea.

"My lord asked how you are this morning, my lady," said Fanny, more formally than usual.

"I am—very tired," she said slowly.

"He instructed me to inform you that it might be well for you to remain in bed today." Fanny did not look at her mistress, busily folding up garments. She must have seen the torn dress in the sitting room, thought Pamela.

"I think I shall." She slid down into the wide bed again, and closed her eyes. But she could not sleep. She went over and over the events of the previous day and night. But she was not sorry for her actions in helping Carlo. He was worthy of help, and his cause was right. She would never apologize for that, though it might ruin her reputation!

And she did not intend to tell Douglas about the incidents. She had promised Carlo to keep silent, and she would.

She slept a little through the day, refusing food, feeling half sick with her anger and pain. She finally got up for tea and did not realize until she was dressed that she wore the warm blue velvet dress with gold banding on the sleeves, and a small thistle pattern in the neck and hem. She was on the point of changing when Fanny told her they were waiting for her in the drawing room.

She shrugged, and went downstairs. She paused at the door of the drawing room, surveying everyone warily. Roger looked nervous and pale. The Signora looked calm and detached, as usual. Douglas? He seemed unusually calm, seated in a satin chair near the Signora. They seemed to have been conversing about something.

Douglas rose on seeing her, and came over to her. He took her right hand, and held it briefly. "Is your arm better, my dear?" he asked quietly. His green eyes were so keen, she thought he could see right through her.

It was not. It burned and throbbed where he had twisted it. "I am all right," she said, and pulled her right hand from his and went around him into the room.

She sank down into a chair on the other side of Signora Margotti. "Will you pour tea this afternoon, Signora, please?" she asked.

"Certainly," said the Signora, and seated herself at the tea table. She began to chatter lightly about the flowers, how they had been touched by frost the night before. "It is coming on to winter, and it will be a cold one, I hear. We might even have some snow. It is seldom that we have snow in Italy, except in the mountains, of course."

Douglas came back to his chair, and took up the mundane theme of the weather with his calm deliberation of manner. So the afternoon went quietly. Douglas did not try to engage Pamela in personal conversation, but he glanced at her occasionally as though judging her mood or feelings.

"I thought tomorrow we might go down to Florence. There is an afternoon concert you might enjoy, Pamela. A pianist, with a concert of classical music. Would you like to sketch for a time first?"

She hesitated. She would like that, and it was a pleasant change from the furious interview and questions she had expected. "Yes, I should like that. Signora, will that plan suit you?" She asked her deliberately, not wanting to be alone with Douglas.

"I am at your delightful command," said the Signora, smiling. She handed a small plate of cakes to Pamela. Pamela reached out with her left arm, winced, and had to refuse it. Douglas at once got up, went to the Signora, took the plate and brought it to Pamela.

He set the plate on a small table beside her. "Thank you," she said in a low tone. She avoided Roger's worried stare and the Signora's involuntary surprise. Douglas sat down beside her.

"You might be interested in the background of the pianist," he said, and proceeded to tell her the training and specialties of the artist. He seemed anxious to please her, but she would not melt toward him. He had infuriated her, distrusted her, insulted her, hurt her physically. A few kind words flung at her would not move her.

She returned to her room after tea, saying she

had letters to write. She sat long over a letter to Adelaide, reluctant to complain, too full of hurt and fury to write platitudes. She ended up writing an empty banal letter of little content.

The next day, Douglas made no attempt to question her. They left early in the day to go to Florence. He took her to an art gallery where a special exhibit was arranged, then sat with her in a café while she sketched. He had planned dinner at a restaurant they all enjoyed, and seemed concerned that she should enjoy every dish.

After lunch, she sat in the restaurant and sketched again, rather nervously, for something to do. Douglas left them for ten minutes, returning with a huge bouquet of flowers which he put at her hand on the table.

She reached out involuntarily for the bouquet, and lifted it to gaze at it in delight. It was a huge bunch of purple violets, and in the center a few small pink rosebuds. "Oh, how exquisite," she murmured, and lifted them to her nostrils. The Signora smiled her approval.

She carried the bouquet with her to the concert, which was delightful. The classical music was both exciting and soothing. The pianist was excellent, and from the breathless silence and the excited applause, the audience also thought so. Douglas had bought box seats, and sat behind Pamela, while she and the Signora occupied the front seats. She was very conscious of him behind her in the darkness. When was he going to question her, berate her again? Was he trying to soften her so she would tell him all about Carlo? He was in for a surprise if he thought she would soften so easily, as to forget her promise of silence.

The crowd for the concert was tremendous, with many standing in the gallery. They waited for a time after it ended, then left to get their carriage in the street outside. Douglas set her cloak about her rather tenderly, being careful of her left arm. She leaned back, her eyes closed deliberately, so he would not spoil everything by talking on the way home.

The next day, he was again careful and considerate of her, and she felt the more wary. She felt rather tense also, thinking he would pounce on her, and question her when she was off guard. But he did not.

She sat in the garden in the afternoon, though the late November day was crisp and cold. She loved to gaze at the lush green of the grass and box hedges, the silvery play of the water in the fountain, the brilliant reds and oranges of the late fall flowers. Her arm ached again, and she made no attempt to sketch, holding her cloak about her.

As she sat in the lounge chair, resting, someone's shadow fell over her from behind. She started as someone dropped a late fall rose into her lap. She picked up the yellow flower nervously, and turned about. Douglas stood there, gazing down at her gravely.

"Are you asleep?" he asked. It was a ridiculous question, and she wanted to laugh.

"No," she said curtly. She lifted the rose to her nostrils. She loved the scents of the various flowers. The roses and violets of yesterday were in a blue vase in her sitting room.

"Is your arm well enough for you to go horse-back riding with me tomorrow?"

She hesitated. She did love to ride. "Perhaps—I will see tomorrow morning," she said finally.

"Good." He seated himself on the next chair, and began to speak idly of some work he was doing. "The reports are almost finished. I shall send Roger to Florence, to engage a rider to take them to Rome." He spoke in this vein for a time, then began to speak of the news he was hearing from Vienna. She was interested, in spite of her continuing anger at him. When he talked seriously to her of politics, she could almost like him again.

The afternoon and evening passed pleasantly enough. She was still very much on guard against him, waiting for him to bring up the subject of Carlo, which he did not.

The next day her arm still ached badly. He sent for the carriage instead of the horses, and they went for a drive, just the two of them. Douglas himself took the reins, and said he wished that he had brought the phaeton with them.

"When we return to Rome, you might wish to learn to drive it. Shall you like that, I wonder?"

She had been longing to learn, and she bit her lip to keep from saying that. She was torn between her desire to learn, and her fierce wish to have nothing to do with him. "I don't know," she finally muttered.

He smiled, as though amused at her, and his green eyes were softened. She scowled. "From this point, we have an excellent view of Florence," he said calmly, and pointed with his long whip at the edge of the road. She gazed and gazed, as he held the horses still so she could look. He pointed out various landmarks, which were now becoming familiar to her—the Cathedral, the Palazzo Vecchio, the Bell Tower of Giotto, the old bridge across the brown Arno River.

He turned the horses finally, and started back. The autumn air was turning colder, and the wind had a bite to it. She thought of Carlo, anxiously, as she often did, and wondered if he had found adequate shelter, enough blankets, and if he was well again. She had heard nothing from him, and had not seen the boy Paolo.

That evening, Roger returned from his mission in Florence and brought back some reports and several packages. He and Douglas were closeted in the study for two hours before dinner. Pamela and Signora Margotti were awaiting dinner when the two men finally returned to the drawing room.

Douglas came up to Pamela, with a small box in his hand. He opened it, set the box beside her, and dangled a locket and chain before her. "Do you like this?" he asked casually, with a slight smile.

She took it reluctantly into her hand. The chain was cleverly wrought of twists of gold, soft and smooth to the touch. The locket was an oval with a cameo of softest pale orange tortoiseshell, the face in creamy white. The profile was of a Greek goddess. "The goddess of love, I believe," said Douglas casually. "Aphrodite. Isn't she lovely?"

"Yes—lovely—" She started to hand it back. He took it from her, hesitated, then slipped the chain about her neck very gently, and settled the locket at her breast. She drew back involuntarily at the touch of his fingers on her dress, and he caught the gesture. His face shadowed. "Thank you," she said very formally, her tone cold. Did he think to soften her with flowers and gifts, and his valuable attentions?

"How pretty against your red velvet dress," commented the Signora chattily. "That is one of our favorite colors here in Italy. That deep red, and that gold—exquisite."

"Pamela looks lovely in any color, though I like her best in blues and the violet shades," Douglas commented, as coolly as though he was discussing art or politics.

Pamela's cheeks stung with color. She hated him. He had every advantage—she could not fight with him in front of Roger, the Signora, and the servants. She felt such a passion and fire, she could not understand it. She had never felt such hate, such a burning in her blood, as though she had a constant fever.

She did not know what she ate for dinner, though the food was as delicious as always. She was silent, while the Signora and Douglas carried the conversation. Roger was quiet, too, his face pale and in shadow as he bent to his plate. He did not look at her, he seemed uneasy and unhappy. Had Douglas been taking out his displeasure with his wife on the poor man who performed his secretarial duties? She would not be surprised to learn it.

They retired early, as Pamela pleaded weariness. She went to her room, allowing Fanny to undress her. She put on nightgown and warm robe, and after Fanny left, she sat in the window seat gazing out from the darkness into the moonlit gardens below.

The sound of a door opening made her start violently. She turned around to see Douglas coming into her darkened room. He was wearing his greenish blue robe with a golden thistle pattern on the shoulders. He hesitated, saw her at the window, and came over to her.

She sat frozen, on the alert like a wild animal. When he put his hands on her shoulders, she stiffened.

"Pamela," he said. "We have been strange to each other for too long. We did not use to feel this way. What happened to us?"

"Many years of strangeness," she said coldly. "You are not the person you were. Perhaps you were never as I thought."

"One becomes hard, unwillingly," he said, and drew her up into his arms. She began to fight him, angrily.

"No—don't! I don't want—"

His mouth crushed down on hers, yet his arms were not so hard and cruel as they had been. He held her silent, while his hands moved slowly up and down her back. She felt an involuntary thrill of response, and hated herself for it. She kicked at him.

"Don't fight me," he whispered, and pulled her closer to him, so she felt the warm lean strength of his body through his robe.

She tried to kick out at him again. Her soft slippers made no impact at all. He picked her up bodily, and carried her across the wide room to the bed.

"No, don't—don't!" she said furiously, her arms flailing out. "Are you going to hurt me again?"

He did not answer. He had removed his robe, and in alarm she saw his intent. She sat up, trying to slide off the bed. He was there in an instant, pushing her back against the mounds of soft cushions. He pressed her down into them, and she felt smothered, incapable of moving between the softness of the bed and the hardness of his lean body with only the nightshirt on it.

He unfastened her robe and put his hands on her nightgown. She wriggled, squirmed, tried breathlessly to protest until his mouth covered hers again with a passionate strength that took her breath away.

Then he was caressing her with his hands and lips. He did not speak again. Her protests were broken, angry, but weakening. He did not listen, did not pay attention to her pleading.

But he did not hurt her. He was careful with her as with a furious child, holding her gently but firmly. And his lips and his hands were caressing, melting away her strength and her will to fight.

She lay limply, and he put her under the covers. There in the darkness and warmth, he took her slowly, gently, but with force.

When it was finally over, she felt dazed, numb, strange. She lay under his arm, as he lay back, breathing hard. So *this* was what it meant—to be a wife. *This* was what he would do to her—time and again.

She hated herself that she had felt thrilled and excited, that her heart had pounded fiercely under his, that her mouth had reluctantly responded to the pressure of his lips. She hated it that she had given in so weakly and submitted to the pressure of his body, until he had had her completely.

He turned her so that her head lay on his shoulder. Slowly he stroked her hair, letting his fingers glide through the strands, stroking her neck, her shoulders, up again to her head. She felt as though she could not move, she had no will left. He bent over her again and kissed her lips softly, as though he now owned them.

He possessed her, he would never let her go, she thought. She was trembling. He drew up the blankets again, to cover them both, and turned on his side, to hold her closely against him.

"Sleep now," he whispered. "Pamela, sleep now —in my arms." And he held her closely against him, her face against his shoulder.

She did not think she could sleep. But the next thing she knew, it was much later. She had wakened a little, to feel his lips on her cheek, on her mouth. She responded sleepily, in a daze, and felt him settle her more closely again on his shoulder, against his body. Then she drifted into sleep again.

In the morning he was gone, but the imprint of

his body was on the bed, the pillows were indented where his head had lain, and the blankets were still warm from his warmth. She sat up, blushed violently, and pushed back her hair. Why had she not kept on fighting him?

Had she been afraid of him, afraid he would hurt her? Had she submitted because she did not want her arm twisted again? No, she had to tell herself, it was not because of that. He had made her feel such strange, violently thrilling emotions that she had wanted to keep on feeling them. Curiosity had driven her on, made her rest weakly in his arms letting him do as he pleased with her body.

She was embarrassed to face him again. She did not want to go down to breakfast. But she must. She got up when Fanny came, and when the maid set out the blue velvet dress she did not correct her.

When she met him in the breakfast room, they were alone. But he was calmly, almost maddeningly casual.

"It is necessary for me to go down to Florence this morning, Pamela. Would you and the Signora like to accompany me? I shall be busy all morning, but we can meet for luncheon."

She hesitated. She did not want to be friendly with him—but how to resist him? And she *did* want to go to Florence.

"Very well," she said finally. The Signora came in, and Pamela informed her of the plans.

"Oh, *bene!* Very good! We might look for the new fabric this morning, my lady. You wished another dress in the brocade, did you not?"

"I hope you are buying blue brocade," said Douglas, with a little smile. "Or a light purple, like the violets, Pamela. Will you consider it?"

She smiled tentatively in response, her gaze sliding away from his. "Oh—I might," she said lightly, teasingly.

"Lilac is your best color," said the Signora. "With your blond hair and violet eyes. My, how they are praised in Italy, you have heard them, my lord?"

"Constantly," said Douglas, with a little grimace. "But you should know, she is also praised in England. When she was just launched in society, the gazettes were always speaking of the beautiful Lady Pamela Ilchester, and whatever gown she had worn at someone or other's ball! I assure you, there was nothing much else to read in the papers!"

"He is teasing. I was rarely mentioned," said Pamela, though she felt flattered. "And how did you see the gazettes, sir?"

"Oh, I often read them when I was laid up after my wounds," he said lightly. "My fiancée was the subject of the warmest praise."

She felt some surprise and a tinge of regret, thinking of the months when he was lying injured in his London house. She had gone over several times with Adelaide, but he did not seem pleased to see her, and she had felt too shy of him to persist. Had he truly thought of her and been pleased that she was praised? Or was he only making conversation?

But Douglas seemed to have set the tone of their new relationship—tentatively friendly, cautious. He took them to Florence with him when he had the time. He paid attention to her conversation in the drawing room and at dinner. He did not come again to her room, but she was much aware of the unlocked door between their bedrooms. She thought he would come again, whenever he pleased. And she did not know how she would react to that.

CHAPTER THIRTEEN

In early December, the flowers froze and the gardens turned to a somber dark hue. Still Florence was fascinating, and when the sun shone in the vivid blue sky, or the stars twinkled brilliantly in the purple night sky, Pamela wanted to gaze and remain in the beautiful place forever.

Then one morning Douglas came to her in her drawing room, interrupting her as she sat writing a letter to her sister. He tapped briefly, and entered. She turned about in surprise.

"I beg pardon for bothering you, but the news is urgent," he said, with a slight worried frown. "I have received a dispatch. I must return to Rome as soon as possible."

"Oh—" Her breath caught, as she gazed up at

him. "Do you mean, we will remain here—"

His frown darkened. "Of course not! You will accompany me. I am sorry we must leave Florence—you do like it, I believe."

"Yes, very much." She turned, to gaze down unseeingly at the papers before her. She had known the fury of anger, the deep worry over Carlo, then the exciting, frightening conflict with her new husband, besides the loveliness of Florence itself.

"How soon can you be ready to leave with me?"

She thought, biting her lip. "Why—whenever you wish, sir. I think Fanny and I can pack everything in one day. The luggage might be sent on later."

"Let us say, then, the day after tomorrow. That will be soon enough." He paused, turned, then said, "Thank you, Pamela. I knew I could count on you." And he went out.

She felt a little strange. Did he think she would throw a scene, have a tantrum on leaving? She did not know him and he did not know her, it seemed.

She rang for Fanny, gave instructions, then went to find Signora Margotti. The woman took the news calmly, but a little frown of worry wrinkled her eyebrows.

"Is it—is it bad news, my lady?" she asked diffidently. "I have had the impression, the feeling—"

"I do not know, Signora. It is something political, I believe, but my lord did not inform me."

"Of course, of course," and she gave a heavy sigh. "My poor Italy, she is doomed for more suffering, I fear," she said absently. "I will be ready, naturally, whenever you wish to leave, my lady."

"Thank you, Signora. May I say that I have enjoyed your companionship immensely? You have helped me enjoy and appreciate Florence." Pamela smiled at the little brisk woman.

The Signora thanked her, emotion choking her voice. Pamela returned to her rooms to direct Fanny, then to see to the packing of the household goods. She was not surprised to find Roger busily packing up papers and dispatches—boxes of them—and directing their loading into crates.

The household was in something of a turmoil, but they managed to have meals and tea as usual, and to get their sleep. Then on the appointed morning, they set out once more. Pamela looked back over her shoulder, a long lingering look, as the carriage rolled down the lane from the villa.

"We shall return to Florence again one day, Pamela," said Douglas quietly.

"Yes, perhaps," she said, and sank back against the cushions. She gazed out thoughtfully at the scenes before them as the carriages rolled down the hills, around the curves—now revealing, now concealing—the view of Florence in the valley below. Her lovely Florence, with its red roofs, creamy and golden buildings, its gaiety and music and art and charm. She hated to leave.

Their return journey was rapid. They stopped on two evenings at the homes of friends, but the evenings were cut short by their own weariness. They were back in Rome all too soon, and unpacking at Douglas's villa.

Adelaide had received the hasty note from Pamela, and the new Italian housekeeper had everything in readiness. The next few days were full, however. She became acquainted with Douglas's staff, found her way about the kitchens and linen rooms, and took control, for the first time of her own household.

She took pleasure in planning meals which Douglas would enjoy, of having tea ready and hot when he came in wearily from another futile round of diplomatic visits. She knew from the look on his face that matters were not going to his liking. He did not discuss politics with her now as apparently there were some secret negotiations going on.

She respected his silence, tried to keep things smooth at home, and waited. He seemed to have little time for her now.

One day he informed her he would be gone all that morning and afternoon. She felt free to go into the city, to the artists' section, to sketch once more. It seemed years rather than weeks since she had last gone.

She was walking down the street with Signora Margotti at her side, glancing at one café and another, trying to decide where to settle at her work, when she saw the phaeton.

"Why, that is—that is his phaeton," she said, half to herself. It was in front of a dim café. She frowned. Had Douglas planned to meet her here? To surprise her? It was one of her favorite places.

Impulsively, she pushed open the door, the warm, steamy air of the café rushing to greet her. The proprietor in his white apron bowed low before her. She smiled.

"A table in the back," she said in Italian. He bowed again, beamed, and began to conduct her back.

Signora Margotti caught at her arm, in an unprecedented gesture. "Please, my lady—no!" she whispered.

Pamela turned about in surprise, then saw where Signora Margotti was looking. Her heart seemed to stop beating, and she froze.

Douglas was there—tall, red-haired, unmistakable. And he was at a small table, leaning forward, his head almost touching the smooth black hair of—Beata Lanza. Beata, radiant in a red velvet gown, her cloak tossed back, her black eyes shining, gazed up at her escort.

Pamela turned about and walked out the door. When she reached the street, she was shaking violently. Signora still held her arm tightly, now aiding her.

They walked a little way down the street. Pamela was so stunned she could not think. This—this was why Douglas had returned to Rome! Douglas, there with his mistress, his Italian mistress. He had been anxious to return to her.

This was his urgent business. This was his secret mission. Beata Lanza!

Pamela felt hot, then cold, burningly furious, then aching with pain. She walked on, her eyes fixed ahead, scarcely seeing where she went. Signora Margotti hung on to her, like a tugboat to a schooner, holding her, protecting her with her slight fierce strength.

Why did she feel like this? So betrayed?

Because I love him, she thought. Oh God, he made me love him—all over again. The aching, blind devotion of my childhood, the awakening passion of the young girl, and now the raging fury of the woman who had been possessed—and discarded. He did not really want her. He had been furious with her.

But she loved him, loved him, with all the passion in her being. He had wakened her to what it meant to be a woman—only to discard her. For Beata Lanza, once more. He had been meeting her there at the café, an obscure café, a rendezvous for lovers!

"My lady—here," whispered Signora Margotti, and helped her seat herself inside a café in the artists' section. Pamela glanced about in surprise. She had not realized she had walked in that direction. Their coachman had followed with the carriage, and waited in the street near the door.

The Signora ordered for them both, imperiously. Pamela sipped at the hot coffee the waiter brought and nibbled at a roll without tasting it.

Then the Signora leaned forward toward her ear. "Do not turn about, my lady. Carlo da Ponte followed us here. He wishes to speak to you. He is at the table behind us. Lean back, if you will."

Pamela felt caught in a nightmare. She had never felt so unready to engage in intrigue. Her heart burned, her head was whirling with the sickening knowledge of her husband's infidelity. She did not want to see anyone, talk to anyone. She wanted to hide in her room, bury her face in a pillow—

"My lady," came the anxious whisper behind her.

She gazed straight ahead, and tried to compose herself. "Yes, Carlo. How goes it with you?" she asked quietly.

"Well, for me. I am healed, thanks to God and to you. But I have news, bad news. I have just discovered—"

A waiter came near them and Carlo paused, sinking behind his newspaper. Pamela spoke quietly to Signora of nothing at all, and the Signora responded casually.

The waiter left them. Carlo leaned forward once more, and his careful whisper just reached Pamela.

"I was at the café where—my lord was. He is meeting with Beata Lanza. My lady, she is trying to make him a traitor! She is trying to find out British secrets from him. He is wary, but he has revealed too much to her. He trusts her family, therefore her."

She felt frozen, incredulous. Beata—a *traitor?* Beautiful, spoiled Beata, of the magnificent, loyal, Lanza family? The family Douglas trusted, because he had fought beside them?

"You are—sure, Carlo?" she muttered.

"*Sure.* I had thought before, but could not believe. I have been tracing the leaks of information. They go to your husband, to Beata Lanza. Also, she has acquired much money and some jewels. Not from lovers, I have learned that. But from men who paid her to give them information."

"My dear God," whispered the Signora, crossing her heart rapidly. "God keep us from such!"

"Amen," whispered Carlo. "Listen, my lady, you must find a way to warn your husband! He will believe you—"

I wonder if he would, Pamela thought. Believe

me, when I am so jealous of Beata?

"There is a link between what my lord knows and what has been revealed by spies. This link must be the woman, Beata Lanza. I followed them today and listened to their conversation. She teases him, talks to him until he unwittingly reveals some little fact—oh God, she will ruin us all! She knows the names of several Italian patriots. They must flee to England, or to Spain—"

Carlo went on whispering, pausing as a waiter or a patron came too close. Pamela felt more and more frozen as Carlo revealed the extent of the betrayal. And all the leaks were being traced to her husband!

"He trusts them too much. He is slow to trust, but when he does, he is too confident. You must warn him, my lady! He will listen to you—"

"What if he will not? He does not trust me very much! He discovered me the night I returned from helping you, when Roger Saltash and I helped you move—" She whispered the words with pain, remembering the violent scene, his fury, the way he had hurt her.

"Ah, I am sorry, so sorry! Shall I speak to him? I would not cause you a moment of concern. And to spoil your marriage, your reputation—dear God, what have I done to you?"

There was a long pause as a waiter reset the table nearby, humming lightly from some opera tune. Finally he moved away.

Pamela murmured, "Do not be concerned. We have known each other from childhood. I think he does not truly mistrust me. I will try to speak to him about this—this woman. I will do what I can about it."

"Ah, thank you. But if you wish, I will come to your husband, convince him that you aided me in my cause—in my despair—that you were a lady of mercy and goodness to me—"

"Hush," said Signora Margotti sharply. "One comes—you must go, Carlo!"

A dark, heavyset man had paused at the door of the café. Carlo slid away out the back, and the man came in to glare about suspiciously, to stare at Pamela rudely. Pamela looked down, got out her sketching pad, and began to sketch the front window of the café, where a white cat sat yawning in the sunshine beside a pot of red geraniums. The heavyset man came near the table, glanced at her work, frowned, and settled down near them.

Finally she stopped, when her fingers ached because she had been holding her hand tightly over the pad.

"Signora, let us leave," she said lightly. "I am not in the mood for work today. If we hurry, we can be home in time for some hot tea and biscuits. Rome is unexpectedly cold today."

"Yes, Italy can turn quite cold, my lady," said the Signora. She stood up eagerly and helped Pamela into her cloak and hood. "You will find that January is quite brisk with the winds." And they went out the door together.

In the carriage, the Signora said quietly, "You may wonder at me, my lady. I do what I can also —for the cause. If you wish to discharge me—"

"I do not wish anything of the sort." Pamela put her white-gloved hand on the small lady's hand. "I honor and respect you. But do not tell me too much, not unless you must. Too many knowing secrets, that is not good."

"Thank you, my lady." She leaned back—a small and fragile, but determined lady—and clasped her hands tightly together in the darkness of the carriage.

They were silent on the way home, each with dark thoughts, heavy worries. The Signora was probably thinking about her poor torn Italy.

And Pamela? She was worrying about how to warn Douglas. Would he believe her? Or would he think she was merely jealous of Beata—which she was.

But she believed Carlo da Ponte. He was a man of honor, a clever, intelligent man. He would be sure of his facts, that Beata was betraying her family and her country, making use of her family's friendship with Douglas to learn secrets and then selling them!

For money and jewelry, said Carlo, and he would know.

If this was the sort of woman she was, Douglas should know that, thought Pamela. But how to tell him? How to convince him that the woman he obviously adored was a traitor, stealing secrets from him to sell to enemies?

Would he guess that Pamela herself was in love with him? That would be the final humiliation, she decided, pressing her hand to her breast. It hurt there, hurt badly. That she should love a man who treated her like this, who despised and forgot her.

CHAPTER FOURTEEN

Douglas seemed absorbed in dark thoughts at dinner. He scarcely seemed to notice Pamela or the others at the table. After dinner, he curtly summoned Roger to his study, and they were closeted there for almost three hours.

Pamela despaired of speaking to him that evening, and finally retired before they emerged from the study. She allowed Fanny to undress her, and then dismissed her.

She was pacing slowly in her room, back and forth, over to the windows, when she heard the doors in Douglas's rooms opening and closing. She paused at the long windows and stared out into the moonlit gardens. They were dim, but she knew the autumn flowers had withered, the box hedges were turning reddish and brown, the fountain had been turned off for the winter. And there was a cold chill, a frightened chill, in her heart as well. It was so lonely to love and not be loved in return!

She began pacing again. She must not think of her love. She must think about Carlo—how to tell Douglas about Beata and her betrayal. She might be wrecking his mission, and he did not know it.

She drew her warm, woolly robe about her and shivered. What could she do? Would Douglas believe her, or turn from her in that red-haired fury of his that she dreaded? She brushed back her long, loose hair with her nervous hands, and paced again, back and forth, back and forth. She could not seem to think clearly.

At a sound from the door, she started violently, and turned. Douglas stood there, dimly outlined against the candle-glow from his own bedroom.

"Pamela?" he said questioningly, and came forward toward her. She stiffened. It was as though her thoughts of him had summoned him. But she could not speak. He loomed over her.

He took her shoulders in his hands, drawing her slowly, gently to him. She tried to hold back. But he drew her against him, held her to his warm, strong body. He tilted back her head with his hand in the warm masses of her blond hair.

"No," she said. "No, I—don't—want—"

Her protests were smothered under his lips. There was a long silence as he kissed her, slowly, savoring her mouth, turning his head slowly to brush his mouth against hers, then drinking deeply again of her parted lips.

She wanted to fight him, but she seemed drained of the will to resist him. He kissed her, then drew her slowly toward the bed. He removed her robe, and she slid under the blankets. She was trembling when he got in beside her, and turned to take her in his arms.

She made one last protest. "Douglas, please—I don't want this—"

He paid no attention. His arms were about her, he drew her to him. His mouth came down, still gently, but with a sure command she could not fight. One hand began moving slowly over her soft body, awakening tremors of delight at his caresses.

Why tonight? she thought. Why tonight, just after she had seen him at a secret rendezvous with his mistress? Why tonight, when she was so concerned about the betrayal of his mission? Why tonight, when she was upset about her love for him, when she feared to tell him the news—why, why should he come to her, and begin making love to her?

She could not tell him about Beata now. He

would be enraged, whenever she told him. And she feared his strength if he turned against her. He would be sorry afterward, yes, but he was like a tiger when he was roused. She knew the story of the Kinnairs in battle, how they went mad with the fighting, and killed and did not know what they did until later. Scotland was full of such stories.

She had no wish to rouse the tiger in him. Not now, especially, she thought, as she trembled with delight at his skilled caresses. She turned towards him involuntarily and gripped his shoulder with a shaking hand. Her breath was coming rapidly through her parted lips, and she was hot and chilled by turns.

She hated her weakness, that she would yield so readily to him. But she loved him, she knew that now, and she wanted him, his strength against her body, his desire beating against hers, demanding response. She sighed, and yielded.

When he lay back beside her, they were both limp for a time from the violence of their reaction to each other.

He seemed to sleep, he lay so still beside her, his arm over her, his face against her shoulder. She closed her eyes, savoring the long moments of peace. Her cheek was against his hair, she could smell the special scent that was his hair, his skin, *him*.

She slid off into sleep herself, so easily that she did not know she had been asleep until she wakened sometime later. He was still with her, now holding her with his arms as she slept with her back curled into his body, his legs supporting hers.

She stirred, sighing, wakening, and he stirred also. His lips brushed against her shoulder. There was no urgency in it, no rough demand, only a gentle caressing, a brushing against her, that soothed and comforted her. She felt at peace, protected, sheltered, as though nothing could ever hurt her again.

She slept again, feeling the curious contentment and surprise of being so happy with him. It was so—*unexpected*, she thought sleepily, curling more tightly against him.

He was gone when she awoke in the morning. She thought she remembered his leaving, just as she was wakening. The bed was still warm from his body. She stretched luxuriously, slowly, her arms brushing the bed, the sheets and pillow where he had lain with her.

She would have to talk to him about Beata. She frowned, sighed. She should have spoken of it last night, but she could not. And when she did bring up the subject, he would probably be furious, and it would shatter the peace between them. She rang for the maid, and got up.

She bathed and dressed in the blue muslin he especially liked. Her lips tightened with something like anger at herself as she realized she was deliberately trying to please him. That she should reach such a pass! Oh well, she was a married woman now, and that was what women had to do—

Please a man.

Her lips smiled, unconsciously, as she met her gaze in the mirror. Fanny was brushing out the long blond curls, and shaping the waves deftly. Would she like to please him? Would she like him to gaze at her across a room, and want her, and come toward her, and take her into his arms— and—

"Are you cold, my lady? You are shivering." Fanny spoke anxiously.

"A little cool today. Rome is colder than I had thought," Pamela responded, her color heightening.

"It surely is, my lady. Why, the water was frozen in the jugs this morning. Had to break the ice before I could pour it out. And I thought England was cold! But the sunshine is nice today."

Pamela was late going down to breakfast. She had overslept. Douglas was already in his study, so was Roger. She ate alone, though Signora Margotti would have been happy to linger over coffee and chatter. Pamela shook her head.

"I must think," she said simply. The Signora nodded, and gazed at her sympathetically before leaving the room.

She broke another slim crescent of roll, buttered it, and ate it with her steaming hot coffee and milk. The dining room was pretty with its blue and white china, the tall vases on the shining polished wood of the buffet and the long dining table. Her gaze went beyond the vases to the soft white and crimson drapes at the French windows, beyond to the gardens where the box hedges shone in their military precision.

It was such a lovely December morning. The sky was so blue and the sun shone warmly, though it was chilly outside. She longed to put on a cloak and go outside and sketch, and forget everything —especially spying and politics.

She heard Roger's voice in the hall, then her husband's deeper tones. She stiffened. Roger was leaving, going on some errand. When he left, she must speak to Douglas alone.

The doors closed, the voices ceased. She finished her coffee nervously, then rose.

She crossed the shining parquet floor of the hallway, across the precious French rugs in blue and cream and rose, and tapped at the door of her husband's study.

"Come in," he called. She opened the door timidly.

His gaze seemed to leap to her as she shut the door after her. His eyes seemed bright green today, shining and unguarded. She forgot for a moment what she had come to say, and he rose and came around the desk.

"Pamela? Come in," he repeated. He held out his hand to her. "What is it? Errands, shopping, sketching?"

"No, nothing like that. It is—something serious, Douglas," she said, with an intense effort.

He gazed down at her, his eyes darkening as he studied her face. "Sit down." He indicated the sofa near his desk. He seated himself on a large straight chair near her after she had nervously arranged her blue muslin skirts on the sofa.

"What is it, then?" he asked, when she was silent. She was searching for how to begin. She had not planned this. She had been too busy trying to get up enough courage to speak at all.

She blurted out, "I was—sketching in Rome yesterday. I mean—I started out with Signora Margotti—"

"And there was trouble?" He frowned as she paused nervously. "I have warned you not to go, Pamela. I really think that—"

"No, no, that is not the matter. I mean, I saw your phaeton in front of a café, and I—I went inside with Signora. And you were there with Beata—"

"*What!*" He stared at her, his face flushing. He was very stiff and erect now. "What the devil do you mean by that, Pamela?"

He was already angry. She shook, and her slim hands pleated the muslin skirt.

"That—that is not what I was concerned about. I mean, it is your own business whom you wish to meet, although I—I mean—"

"It meant nothing!" he said. "I have told you she is a friend of long standing. I fought with her father and brothers, and she is a fine woman of a good reputation! I am surprised at you, Pamela. You are probably listening to gossip—"

"No, I came to warn you," she finally interrupted him, simply. "She is a spy, a traitor. What you have told her is being given as information— against your mission here. She is betraying her own family."

Her large violet eyes met his blazing, incredulous green ones directly, bravely. She could see he did not believe her.

"I have been warned by one I trust," she went on, when he did not speak. "Beata Lanza has managed to learn some secrets from you, and she—"

"She has learned *nothing* from me!" he said curtly. He raised his large right hand firmly, and the fist clenched. "Nothing. My God, Pamela, if you think I am easily duped—"

"She has learned enough to betray your mission.

That is why secrets have leaked out, spoiled the plans you were making. I know it, Douglas. Be warned! You cannot trust her! She is betraying her own cause for money and jewels. The person who told me—"

"Carlo da Ponte? Is that it? You have been seeing him again! I warned you, Pamela, I will not have you—"

"He is a fine, courageous man! He takes his life in his hands to warn me about it! I promised to approach you on the matter!" She was now becoming angry. He was so infatuated with Beata that he could not believe her, when he had known her all his life!

"Then he is deceiving you for his own motives! You cannot trust him!"

"I would trust him with my life!" she shot back angrily.

"And you have, eh? Have you met him often since we returned to Rome?" He caught at her wrist, and held it tightly as she shrank from him. "I warn you, Pamela, you drive me mad! I will not have you meeting anyone secretly! Your reputation, your honor—"

"—is safe with Carlo!" she raged. "Let me go, Douglas! You are hurting my wrist!" She braved him with her eyes, holding still with an intense effort.

He loosened his grip, but did not let her go.

"He lies about Beata. He means to make trouble! She is a fine, honorable person! I have entrusted my life to her father and *he* never betrayed me! I owe him my life, and now you say his daughter would betray us all! And I have told her nothing—"

"You have let slip pieces of information, Douglas—Carlo has said so," she said more quietly. "She puts things together, cleverly. Little facts add up."

"He lies," he said flatly, the color staining his cheeks. His green eyes were hard as ice. "He knows nothing about my mission!"

"I believe he knows everything about your mission, Douglas. He wishes it to succeed, he is trying to help. But Beata Lanza is betraying it—and you! She may be your mistress, but—"

"My—*what!*" His fingers tightened cruelly on her wrist and he glared down at her. "You dare to say that! She is a good woman, I have not—"

Her mouth was tight. "All Rome knows she is your—lover," she said coldly. "And I have eyes. I have seen you together. Do not deceive me, Douglas, or think I am easily fooled. What you do is your own affair, but do not try to tell me what to believe!"

Her own words stung her. He flung her wrist from him, and stood up to pace about the study furiously. She watched him, rubbing her wrist gently where he had hurt it. He flung about and said, "It is all lies! I *cannot* believe you. Are you so jealous of me that you make up such stories—"

She stood up, pulling her dignity about her with an effort. "As I said, what you do is your own concern," she said with cold hauteur. "I came to warn you about the mission, and not to trust her with any conversation on politics. She is evidently clever enough to put small facts together and sell some secrets. That is all."

He came over to her and blocked her path as she would have left the room. They glared at each other, neither giving way.

"You must take my word for it, that Beata is a fine woman," he said slowly. "She would not betray. But as for Carlo da Ponte, he will use lies and any method to achieve his goals! I forbid you to see him again! I will not have you meeting him secretly—"

While he would meet Beata Lanza when and where he chose, she thought bitterly. "I do not believe you, and you cannot believe me. It is an impasse, is it not?" she said quietly, with bitter anger.

"You must believe me! You are my wife, and you must do as I say! Believe me, Pamela," he said, more gently, "you are only a child, you are much younger than I. You are involved in something you cannot possibly understand. The intrigues and fictions of governments, the spying and lying that must go on—you cannot possibly comprehend what is happening."

"I understand, and I am no longer a child," she

said with dignity. "You forget—I am grown up. I will not be bullied, or told to ignore what is under my nose! Nor will I believe what I am told to believe, when it is contrary to what my mind tells me is the truth!"

"You are still a child," he said, his nostrils white with rage. He put out his hand to her impulsively, and she shrank back from him. He saw the gesture, and his hand dropped to his side. He stared down at her. "What has happened to us, Pamela?" he said softly, with an abruptly different tone. "As a child, you trusted me implicitly. What has happened? Where is that child, that trusting gentle child?"

"She grew up, to find betrayal and deceit and lies all about her," cried Pamela, and rushed from the room before he could see the tears gathering in her violet eyes.

CHAPTER FIFTEEN

Pamela was so upset she remained in her room the remainder of the day. She pleaded a severe head-ache, and lunch was sent up to her on a tray.

But there was no message from Douglas, no word that he was sorry. Nor did he come to see her. He must be as bitterly angry with her as she was with him, she figured.

She brooded, and developed a real headache. She finally tried to sleep in order to prepare for a ball that evening in honor of a visiting British dignitary. She was in no mood for it, but it must be attended.

Over and over in her mind went the facts, the quarrel, the puzzlement of what to do. She knew that Carlo had spoken the truth to her. He felt he owed her a great deal, and he had risked his life, his reputation, and his cause to warn her. It *was* the truth about Beata Lanza, and if Douglas did not believe her and went on trusting Beata, the mission was doomed to failure.

Fanny came to her room early in the evening, tiptoeing until she saw that her mistress was awake. "Shall I bring you hot tea, my lady?" she asked solicitously. "My lord asks if you are well enough to attend the ball this evening."

Pamela sat up wearily, pushing back her masses of blond hair. She felt more like weeping. "Yes, of course I shall attend," she said dully. "Inform his lordship I shall be ready at eight. But I think I shall dine here in my room first. Some hot tea and rolls, Fanny, that is all."

Fanny pressed her lips together tightly, and forbore any comment. But from her frown, Pamela knew she was worried. She brought a tray with two soft boiled eggs, as well as the tea. She ate a little, and felt better.

Then Fanny dressed her for the ball in a bluish green gown of satin brocade cunningly embroidered in a pattern of small gold birds and flowers. Her hair was dressed in a new fashion—waves and a single long curl over her shoulder. Fanny brought out the emeralds—the necklace and bracelet and stunning, huge ring—which Pamela put on in silence.

The Kinnair emeralds. She had heard about them all her life, and when they became engaged she had thought that one day she would wear his jewels proudly. Now she felt nothing but a dull despair. He hated her, despised her, distrusted her.

On an impulse, when Fanny was out of the room, she took out the golden thistle brooch she had not worn for weeks. She fastened it under the dress, safely inside, on her undergarment. It might bring her luck once more. What luck, she could not imagine.

Fanny set a blue velvet cloak about her. "There, love, you look grand," she said in a familiar loving tone. "There'll be no one finer at the entire ball, nay, in the whole of Rome, I'll warrant!"

Pamela smiled faintly. "Oh, there will be many grand ladies there," she said listlessly. She took one last critical look in the mirror, noting how the blues and greens set off her blond beauty, but she took no pleasure in it. Douglas did not. How could she?

She emerged from her room and started down the wide staircase. As though on cue, Douglas came from his study into the hallway, and then to the foot of the staircase to wait for her. He wore his blue green suit with the golden decorations. His head was back, his face taut and controlled.

He was still angry with her. She felt it, coming slowly down the staircase to him.

"You look beautiful," he said formally, taking

her hand on the last two steps. "Are you feeling quite all right again?"

She glanced away. "I still have the headache," she said, in a stifled tone, listlessly. "But I thought it necessary to attend this occasion."

"We can leave early if you like," he said coldly, frowning. He escorted her to the front entrance, saw her settled in the carriage, then got in beside her.

They were silent on the way to the ball. She thought of several trivial topics of conversation and discarded them as not worth the attempt. Douglas would glance at her, frown, then glance away again, gazing out the windows at the darkened streets.

At the villa they were greeted by the host and hostess. Pamela prepared to speak Italian the greater part of the evening, knowing she was much appreciated for her efforts to speak their language.

Douglas danced with her first, holding her stiffly from him. She was glad when the dance was over, and he turned her over to their host. He was full of compliments in fulsome Italian, his gaze lingering on her bare shoulders and the pale skin beneath the emerald necklace. She was glad to dance with Roger Saltash, for he made no attempt to speak. He gave her in turn to an Italian attaché, who moved her on to a Russian aide, and so on and on.

It was quite forty-five minutes before she returned to Douglas. He was standing speaking with some male friend at the side of the ballroom when she came to stand quietly beside him. He glanced down at her keenly.

"Are you feeling better, Pamela? Shall I get some champagne for you?" he asked in a low tone.

She shook her head, attempting to smile at his friend. "No, I shall have a drink later, thank you. How pleasant this room is, all the beautiful flowers. And the mirrors reflecting all, enchanting," she said in Italian.

The friend asked her to dance, then Douglas danced with her again. He was still stiff and formal with her, and it made her feel quite miserable, this strangeness between them, just when they were becoming close in their marriage. It was fated to go wrong, she thought miserably. She should have been quite firm and refused to marry him when she realized how he felt about Beata Lanza.

A waiter brought her a cooling drink Douglas had ordered. She looked up to glance and smile her thanks. Her face froze. She was looking into Carlo's face.

He was tanned beyond recognition, a small black mustache on his upper lip. His hair was dyed black, but she knew him. He stared at her significantly, then lowered his eyes discreetly.

"Thank you," she murmured, and took the glass. He moved away.

Douglas said, "Would you like something to eat, Pamela? The tables are in the next room."

"Thank you, no, not yet." She could not help from watching Carlo as he moved to another couple with drinks. Why was he here? To spy in general? Or was there some significant purpose in his presence? Did he expect something to happen tonight?

"Ah, Beata," said Douglas warmly. "Here you are. I feared you would not be able to attend this evening."

Pamela turned about to meet the flashing black eyes of her rival. The woman was wearing a tightly cut ruby brocade dress with black sequins. Her red mouth was the color of her dress and her cheeks flamed with color. Pamela felt faded and dim beside her, like an old tired portrait.

"Father was ill, I thought I should not leave him," she said in soft, seductive tones. "But he persuaded me to come. My brother brought me. I have not seen you since Tuesday, my friend!"

This last was a murmur in Douglas's ear, but Pamela heard it. She turned cold. Tuesday was only yesterday! Douglas seemed rather flushed and nervous, she thought.

"Ah—yes," he said vaguely. "Pamela, my dearest, you have been acquainted with Alfonso Lanza."

The brother beamed, bowing from the waist, and asked Pamela to dance. She moved away from the other two, feeling bitter and unhappy. She glanced back around Alfonso's shoulder and saw them moving smoothly into the waltz.

And beyond them, Carlo was watching, his eyes narrowed keenly.

When the dance ended, she asked Alfonso Lanza to leave her near Roger Saltash. Roger promptly asked her to dance, then she asked him to leave her near someone else. She talked to dowagers and chaperons, danced with aides and ambassadors and consuls and the wealthy and titled, scarcely knowing who they were. They laughed at things she said, so she must have said something, she thought vaguely. She talked in Italian and English and French and twice in Spanish, which she had not thought she could do.

Still the evening dragged on. She saw Douglas at a distance, frequently with Beata, sometimes with another lady. He would glance in Pamela's direction, frown, his green eyes icy-cold, then move away again.

He did come to claim her for dinner. He took her in to the tables set for the evening, and solicitously helped her to dishes of creamy puddings, salads, meats, iced confections, little sandwiches —anything she wished, and twice as much as she wanted. She sat down with her plate on a sofa near a titled Russian lady, and listened and smiled and heard not a word. Douglas stood nearby, his plate on a convenient mantel, and discussed hunting with a hearty British type.

They returned to the dancing. Pamela was aware of an ache in her heart and in her head. She was in a daze of unhappiness, a trance that seemed to trap her and hold her from reality. If she thought about how miserable she was, she would die, she thought. She must not think. She must dance, and laugh, and chatter about nothing.

She paused once near the doorway, wishing she could slip away and never return. She went out into the hallway, and rubbed her aching head. When someone touched her arm, she started violently.

It was Carlo. "My lady, come with me. We may catch her—quickly!" He was so excited he was shaking.

Pamela went with him without thinking since she trusted him implicitly. He drew her along the empty hallway. She could hear the din of the music, the laughter and chatting fading as they moved farther away from the ballroom.

They went farther, towards the end of the hallway. Cautiously Carlo opened a door, and they stole inside. She stopped, shocked.

Beata Lanza and Roger Saltash were at an open safe. The host's study held a huge safe behind the desk, and they were standing there, examining the papers inside! Roger was handing them to Beata, who was examining them, laying them on the desk, turning back for more. Jewelry was spread out on the desk, in open cases.

At some sound the two turned, lithe, trapped like animals at bay. Beata's black eyes flashed with fury, and Roger stared and dropped a pile of papers, which scattered like white leaves before him.

Carlo dashed at him as Roger reached for the pistol lying on the mantel near his hand. The two men grappled, and Beata backed away from them.

Pamela stood transfixed. Roger! Roger was with Beata in her betrayal! Roger Saltash, the kindly, weak aide of her husband!

"Oh no, *no*—Carlo, be carful!" She cried it out as Roger succeeded in reaching the pistol. Carlo caught at Roger's hand, but his shoulder was still weak, his arm not strong enough to prevent the movement of the pistol. Relentlessly, Roger moved his arm, with the pistol in that hand, moving it to bear on Carlo at close quarters to him.

Behind Carlo, Beata was raising a vase. Pamela dashed forward, caught the woman's arm, and pulled on it sharply. The vase dropped, the angry woman turned on her, and yanked at her hair.

"Help!" Pamela called, again and again. "Help us! Help!" She could see that Carlo was weakening, though she was fighting desperately with Beata. She pulled at the woman's arm, yelping as Beata tugged at her blond hair.

"What is this? What—" Douglas dashed into the room, and she saw him over Beata's ruby shoulder. He was stunned with shock, staring at them, then rushing forward to rescue her as Beata's hands closed on her throat.

Beata fell back as Douglas yanked at her. Pamela reeled from her, gripping at the desk to save herself from falling. She half turned, to see that Roger had turned from Carlo, and was aiming the pistol at Douglas!

"No, no, no," Pamela was muttering. She never knew how she reached Roger. All she knew was that she had to save Douglas. She reached him, gripped the arm with the pistol in the hand. She wrenched it upward, swung off her feet as with unexpected strength he fought her.

Douglas turned, dropped Beata, and lunged at Roger. He wrestled for the pistol, thrusting Pamela away with his arm, urgently, out of range. She leaned panting on the desk, watching with an ache in her heart, and a blur before her eyes, as the man she loved fought for his life. Roger had the gun aimed at Douglas, it was averted only as Douglas fought to press the gun aside. They twisted, turned, bent over it, and the gun went off.

It was a deafening roar in the small room. Douglas staggered back. Pamela screamed, rushing to him. "Douglas—my darling—Douglas!"

She caught at him, but he was only gasping for breath. Roger was falling, falling, and blood was spreading slowly over his white shirt front, his eyes were staring.

Carlo bent toward him.

"Da Ponte—get out fast," Douglas gasped. Carlo nodded, glanced briefly at them, dashed out the French windows to the outdoors.

Pamela leaned limply on a chair, her hand to her throat. It had been so close. Douglas might have been killed. She had felt frozen with horror when he had been in danger. Oh, Douglas, Douglas, I love you so much, she thought. He was bending over Roger as the door of the study burst open and men began to pour in. They stared at the strange sight before them.

Pamela straightened up, began to turn, and saw the ruby-clad arm upraised—too late. Beata Lanza struck Pamela over the head with the vase she held in her strong hands.

The vase struck her full on the temple.

There were lights in the room, sounds, voices, snatches of music from the ballroom, shouts— and then nothing.

She was smothered in a dark veil of gray turning to black, as she fell deeply into a void.

CHAPTER SIXTEEN

It was four days before Pamela had recovered enough from the blow to sit up on the lounge in her sitting room. The violent headache had finally receded, aided by the medicines and long hours of sleep.

Douglas had come in frequently, to gaze down at her in bed, touch her gently, and ask in a low voice how she felt. She was too weak to inquire what was going on. Fanny had informed her that Roger Saltash was under arrest, that when his wound had improved he would be removed to England under guard. She did not know about Beata Lanza and her fate. Carlo Da Ponte had disappeared.

Pamela, even in her daze, felt the keen unhappiness that came from knowing Douglas had loved an unworthy woman. How miserable he must feel. He would hate her all the more, she thought, for revealing such a terrible weakness in his beloved Beata.

There seemed to be no answer for them. Would Douglas divorce her after some decent interval? She supposed so. They could not continue like this, and she turned her face to the wall and closed her eyes, her hand clenching the soft cushions.

The door of the sitting room opened softly. She kept her eyes shut, hoping the person would go away. He did not. He came softly to the lounge, and touched her forehead gently. "Pamela? Are you awake, darling?"

She turned slightly on the lounge, opened her eyes, to gaze up at Douglas.

"I am—awake," she said, with an effort.

"I am sorry to disturb you, but there is someone to see you, and he cannot remain long. Come in, Da Ponte," he said, and beckoned.

Pamela sat up so suddenly that her head started spinning. "Oh, Carlo!" she whispered eagerly, and held out her hand to him.

The serious-faced man came over to her, bent devotedly to her hand, and pressed a kiss on it. "My lady," he said, "how can I thank you? You have saved me yet again."

"You should not have come here! You take too

many chances, Carlo," she scolded gently. Douglas was putting cushions at her back, settling her into the lounge. She sank into the cushions with relief. "Thank you, Douglas. Please sit down, Carlo, but you must not stay long."

"No, no, I cannot. I have to leave Italy, it is arranged. I have been betrayed," he said, his face shadowed. "But I shall manage—do not fear. I shall continue the work elsewhere. I but came to tell my lord the story, to set things right."

Douglas came to sit on the end of Pamela's long lounge and leaned forward intently to listen as Carlo spoke in a low voice of what had been happening.

"Her conspirator was Sir Roger Saltash, as I learned that last evening. He had gambled heavily, lost all his own fortune, taken money from you and lost that. His only chance was to betray, to sell secrets. Then he enlisted Beata Lanza also, and the two of them revealed all they learned from you. That is why your mission was continually betrayed—it never had a chance at secrecy."

Douglas nodded, as Carlo concluded. "So I was doubly fooled. That is a bitter pill, indeed," he said ruefully. "I can face battles, and an enemy. But an enemy in my own house, in my confidence —that is difficult. I shall be wiser, I hope, in the future."

Carlo smiled gently at Pamela, who was listening intently to all they said. "You can trust this lady with your life and your honor," he said quietly. "She is worthy of all your confidence, I can assure you. She will help you and keep silent, though it cost her dear."

"I know that now," said Douglas. Carlo stood up.

"I must leave. Farewell. And my deep gratitude—to you both." He bent once more and kissed Pamela's hand.

"God keep you, Carlo," she said, and pressed his hand tightly with hers.

"May he always keep you safe and happy, my lady," he responded, with a last smile at her.

Then he left, and Douglas went with him. Pamela sank back into the cushions. Douglas had not seemed very upset at the revelations. He must have been learning much the past few days while she lay ill. But perhaps under his cool exterior he was burning with anger and frustration.

The door opened again, and Douglas came in, closing the door after him. She stiffened. Had he come to berate her, to scold? Or to suggest quietly, with deadly cold, that they separate?

She must be ready for anything, she thought, desolation in her heart.

He came over and sat down on the chair beside her. "Pamela, are you strong enough to discuss this? I do not want to weary you unduly."

"Yes, of course, we may as well speak," she said, and folded her hands at her waist. She saw him gaze thoughtfully at her hands on the blue robe.

"Some six years ago," he began unexpectedly, "I was in love, or thought I was in love, with a lady. She was as lovely as you—almost. She was blond and pretty and gay. We became engaged, informally, and I was about to send out the announcements to the gazettes. Then I found her with a wealthy, rather coarse man of some distant acquaintance under compromising circumstances. I confronted her to find that she had been—acquainted rather closely with him for some time."

Pamela's wide violet eyes were gazing at him in startled manner. "Oh, Douglas," she gasped. "How horrid!"

He smiled slightly. "Yes, it was horrid," he agreed. "Quite disillusioning, in fact. I found that the lady was a flirt, a rather cold-blooded one, who was quite well paid for her charming ways. In fact, when she found I was not in direct line for the title, she broke our engagement. I was quite bitter about it, not realizing at the time what a blessed escape I had had. At about this time, your father was gravely ill. He sent for me, asked me to look after you. I agreed to become engaged to you. You were seventeen, very young, very naive, very sweet and trusting, as I thought."

"Oh, I was never naive—never, really!" she protested vigorously. She sat up, but he pushed her gently back into the cushions.

"As you recall, I was sent to the Peninsula, to Spain, under Wellington. I returned, wounded. When I lay in my London house, you came to call. You had changed, I thought. You were in the gazettes, the beauteous Lady Pamela—gaming, racing her horse in the park, frivolous, much sought after—and the manner in which you spoke—"

"I was nervous with you, Douglas. You seemed so serious, so—so ill. I wanted to amuse you," she said in a low tone.

"I realize that now. But I thought you were like the flirt. I was ill—irritable, I suppose. I rebelled at the thought of marriage to you, thinking you had changed from the serious, charming child I had known. I took the mission to Italy, and departed."

"You did not mean to marry me, then. You were going to—to fry off," she said childishly, flushing. "Oh, I wish we had not come to Italy! It pushed you back into the situation. We might have broken the engagement otherwise—"

He captured her nervous hand as it gripped the cushion. "Do you wish you had not come to Italy?" he asked seriously. "I have no such thoughts. As I came to know you again, to realize that underneath your beauty was a serious mind, an intent of purpose, a gentleness and thoughtfulness for others, a deep concern for England and for Italy—"

She was blushing more deeply under his intent gaze. "Oh, but you—you loved Beata, as I learned —and you and she—"

"No, Pamela. You were wrong about that," he said quietly, without anger. "She was never my mistress, nor did I love her as I love you. I admired her, as I had admired her father and brothers. I thought she was of the same caliber. It is a bitter disappointment to learn she is not."

"What—what will they do—with her?"

He did not let loose her hand. "Her father has taken her to their country home, far in the mountains. She will be kept there and questioned about her part in the dealings. He is gravely unhappy with her. He means to be much more firm with her and plans to marry her eventually to some man of his choosing. She was much spoiled."

There was a long silence between them.

"Pamela," he said finally, "I was intensely jealous of you. I thought first that you loved Carlo da Ponte, then Roger Saltash, then I found that I cared only that you did not love me. I was so angry that I was violent with you and hurt you. I cannot forgive myself for that. My damnable temper! The curse of my family. That I should turn my roughness on you!"

A little incredulous hope was rising, bubbling inside her. He said again that he loved her—did he mean it?

"I—I suppose I provoked you," she said slowly.

He began to smile, slowly. "I should think you did!" he said vigorously. "You are the most provoking, maddening, entrancing, devilish, strong-willed female of my acquaintance! And that I should marry you! It served me right!"

This was no romantic declaration. She sat upright, glaring at him. "That is not kind! That is not gentlemanly! You do not like me at all! You could never love me! To speak of me like that!" she raged, quite forgetting her injured head.

"Could we not start over, Pamela?" he asked more seriously, capturing her other hand and pulling her slowly toward him. "I assure you, that in spite of your infuriating ways, I do indeed have very tender sentiments toward you."

He was laughing at her, teasing her as he had when they were young, when she was a girl enamoured by the tall, strong boy with the flaming red hair.

"Oh, Douglas, you do—anger me!"

"Could we not begin again?" he questioned, his mouth very close to hers. "I want to start over, Pamela. I will try to win you."

"No, we can't start over, I don't want to start over," she said, in spite of the weakness stealing over her at his nearness.

"No?" he questioned, his mouth inches away. "Why not, darling? Do you—hate me? I don't think you did the other night!"

"Oh—you—you are—"

"You lay in my arms so sweetly—" he whispered, and his mouth came down hard on hers, capturing, winning easily, as she lay back over his arm. She felt him trembling, even as she was shaking under his caresses. "My love," he murmured, "my love, my darling—" And he kissed her again, more fiercely, forgetting her weakness.

"I don't need to start over, Douglas," she finally confessed, as he released her mouth for a few moments. "I—loved you always. Since I was very small. I love you, I always have—"

He kissed the confession from her lips, demanded to hear it again and again, and the time slipped away as they spoke of the days long ago, the days when they had raced their horses across the hills, and laughed together, and talked.

But this was the present, and they were married, and the boy had grown up, and so had the girl.

"And now you are a woman, Pamela, my wife, and so very dear to me! And if you make me jealous, I shall beat you!"

She traced her finger along the laughing lines of his dark face as he bent over her. "You would —beast," she said, and sighed with contentment.

Dell's Delightful
Candlelight Romances

**The irresistible love story
with a happy ending.**

THE PROMISE

A novel by
DANIELLE STEEL

Based on a screenplay by
GARRY MICHAEL WHITE

After an automobile accident which left Nancy McAllister's beautiful face a tragic ruin, she accepted the money for plastic surgery from her lover's mother on one condition: that she never contact Michael again. She didn't know Michael would be told that she was dead.

Four years later, Michael met a lovely woman whose face he didn't recognize, and wondered why she hated him with such intensity . . .

A Dell Book $1.95

She was driven into womanhood by the
terrible passions that ruled men's hearts.

the Slow Awakening

by **Catherine Cookson**
writing as **Catherine Marchant**

The author of <u>Miss Martha Mary Crawford</u> has created
another passionate and endearing heroine in Kirsten
McGregor, an orphan who had to learn early how to survive
brutal hardships. As a young woman, she was sold into
servitude to a cruel and elderly tinker. The whim of harsh
destiny forced Kirsten to carry the child of her vicious
master and face the threat of death. Worse still was the
secret which prevented her from achieving happiness with
the one man who could awaken her lonely heart! "A
wonderfully engrossing tale. Catherine Cookson-Marchant
casts her usual spell with passions and people, and as always,
her novel ends much too soon."—Publishers Weekly

A Dell Book $1.95